The MYSTERY
of the GULLS

The MYSTERY
of the GULLS

PHYLLIS A. WHITNEY

Illustrated by Janet Smalley

Philadelphia
THE WESTMINSTER PRESS

Contents

CHAPTER

⫷ 1 ⫸

The Girl Who Would Not Wave

IN THE morning sunlight Lake Michigan looked like a huge piece of crumpled tin foil. Taffy Saunders, braced against the breeze that buffeted her and tugged at the long taffy-colored braids that had earned her her nickname, stood at the rail of the lake steamer and watched exciting wedges of green land come out of the north and slip past the boat.

"Isn't it in sight yet, mother?" she called over her shoulder. "Can't we see even a speck of it?"

Mrs. Saunders, reading comfortably in a deck chair, looked up from her book to peer across the water. She was young and slight, almost boyish in her brown gabardine slacks and yellow blouse.

"You can't see from there," Taffy protested. "Oh, do come and look!"

Her mother glanced at the watch on her wrist. "It's too soon for Mackinac. You'll recognize the island by the white walls of the fort."

Taffy sighed. Sometimes grownups could be very difficult. Not only because they wouldn't get excited when you were excited, but for other reasons. The matter of not answering perfectly sensible questions, for instance.

The deck chair next to her mother was vacant and Taffy seated herself on the footrest, put her chin in her hands, and regarded her mother earnestly.

"Mother, when are you going to tell me about the mystery?"

For a few seconds her mother went on reading, as if she weren't going to answer. Then a quirk that was almost a smile lifted the corners of her mouth and she turned the book face down on her lap.

"I wish you wouldn't call it a mystery, Taffy. There's nothing mysterious about it really."

Taffy put on what her father called her "unconvinced face" and waited. Mother could say what she liked, but there *was* a mystery. Again and again Taffy had found herself shut out of the hospital room in Chicago where her father was recuperating from his injuries in an automobile accident. They wanted to talk "business," her parents had explained, so wouldn't she rather go for a walk than sit in a stuffy hospital room? She'd grown quite tired of walks.

The business, Taffy suspected, concerned the matter of Aunt Martha Irwin's queer will, which had left her summer hotel on Mackinac Island so unexpectedly to Taffy's mother. The legacy was unexpected because Aunt Martha had been very much displeased when her niece had married Bill Saunders. Then, a few months ago, she had died and Mrs. Saunders had been notified about the will. As a result, she and Taffy were on their way to Mackinac to spend the summer at Aunt Martha's hotel, Sunset House. But Taffy knew very well that there *was* a mystery and that she hadn't been told all about the will.

"All right," her mother gave in suddenly. "Perhaps it would be better for you to know the facts. After all, I'm going to need your help in a lot of ways, and if you understand, it will be easier for you to help me. Daddy and I would have preferred not to have you worry your head about this, but if you're going to worry anyway and talk about mysteries, you'd better know what it's all about."

"We are going to own the hotel, aren't we?" Taffy asked.

"I hope so. But that's a point that won't be settled finally until September. Aunt Martha liked to do odd, unexpected things, and sometimes it was hard to guess her reasons for the way she acted. In her will she stipulated that the hotel would come to me only if I could manage it successfully myself for one whole summer."

"But that ought to be easy," Taffy said. "You said that most of the guests had made reservations ahead of time and that there was already a housekeeper running everything. So all we need to do is just keep on with it."

Mrs. Saunders nodded uncertainly. "Mm — yes. It sounds easy. But I wish I knew what Aunt Martha had in mind. I hope nothing will go wrong."

"Of course it won't," Taffy assured her stanchly. "But it wouldn't matter too much if it did, would it? We didn't have a hotel before. So we don't have to have one now."

"That's the part I didn't want to tell you," Mrs. Saunders said, after a silence. "I didn't want to have you count

on something and then be disappointed if it didn't work
out."

" Count on what? "

" You understand about daddy's accident — I mean that
he won't be able to go back to his old job that kept us
moving all over the country? "

Taffy nodded happily. She certainly did understand.
Daddy's company had been wonderful. He'd been kept
on the pay roll, and when he was well again in September,
he was to have a good position in the Chicago office. That
meant that for the first time in her memory they could
settle down and have a home in one place. No more hotels,
and apartments, and borrowed houses you had to move
out of when the owners came home. No more two months
here and six months there. She could go to the same school
year after year and keep the friends she made.

" Now that we can settle down," Mrs. Saunders went on,
" we'll want a home of our own. But the hospital and
doctor expenses have taken just about all we had saved.
This hotel would be the answer. If we can sell it, it will
bring enough money so that we can make that new start in
our own home. But I can't sell it unless I own it, and I
shan't own it unless everything goes well this summer."

So that was it. So that was how important Sunset House
had become in the lives of the Saunderses. But of course
everything would go well this summer. What could possibly happen to prevent it? Then the Saunderses would
have their own house — a house with a back yard that
might hold a dog, a house with a room that would be
Taffy's very own.

She could almost see that room when she closed her
eyes. There'd be a ruffly bedspread to match the window
curtains, and a dressing table where she could comb her
hair without having to take turns with mother. Oh, everything *had* to go right at the hotel!

"Well, that's the story," her mother concluded. "And that's why I hope everything will go smoothly. Mrs. Tuckerman, the housekeeper, has been with Aunt Martha for the last ten years. I hope we can depend on her to help us. And I hope you'll get along nicely with her daughter, Donna."

Taffy hoped so too. Donna Tuckerman was one of the reasons she looked forward with interest to the summer on Mackinac Island. It had been so long since she'd had a best friend. Recently, wherever they'd lived there'd been plenty of boys, but no girls her own age. Of course she couldn't be sure Donna would be her age. In her letters Mrs. Tuckerman had never said just how old she was, and it could be that Donna would prove six years old and an awful pest. Or else sixteen and snooty about anybody who was twelve.

Suddenly Taffy took her chin from her hands and sat up straight, regarding her mother with a critical eye.

"Mother, do you think you ought to go ashore dressed the way you are? I mean in slacks?"

Mrs. Saunders looked surprised. "What's wrong with my slacks? I thought you liked them."

There was nothing wrong with them, or with mother in them. In fact, Taffy was sure there wasn't another mother on the boat so young and so pretty as hers. But now she felt a new weight of responsibility in regard to Sunset House.

"Maybe they aren't — well, dignified. For a hotel manager, I mean."

Mother stared at her for a moment and then began to laugh softly. "Oh, goodness! I won't have you going strict with me. Sunset House is a vacation hotel. You'll see everything imaginable in the way of clothes."

"But I remember daddy saying it was an old-fashioned sort of place," Taffy protested. "In slacks you won't look important enough to be the manager of a hotel."

Mrs. Saunders fluffed her bright fair hair above the yellow scarf that bound it. "Old-fashioned is right. Aunt Martha kept it so dignified it hurt. I still remember that from my visits as a small girl. Stop worrying, honey. We're going to do a better job than Aunt Martha ever did. We're going to give Sunset House new life."

She picked up her book again and Taffy returned to the rail to watch the gulls following the ship. From the time the boat had left Chicago the gulls had been fascinating to watch, dipping and gliding and soaring in a sort of rhythmic dance, swooping down on a bit of food churned up in the wake of the boat and screaming in pursuit of the one that captured the tidbit.

What a strange cry they made! When she closed her eyes she could almost imagine the cry was something human. A word they seemed to be calling. She could almost understand it — but not quite.

Absorbed in the gulls, she had paid little attention to the water ahead, and now she saw that a high green mound of island had come into sight. A diagonal line running upward across the mound gleamed white in the bright sunlight. This must be Mackinac!

A boy had come to stand beside her at the rail and he too was looking eagerly toward the green mound. She knew that his name was David Marsh and that he was thirteen years old, because yesterday the ship's magician had called him up in front during a show, to help with some of the tricks, and had asked his name and age.

"Is that Mackinac Island?" Taffy asked.

The boy had curly brown hair and brown eyes, and practically a million freckles. He had seemed nice when he was helping the magician, so it was easy to talk to him.

"That's Mackinac, all right," he said. "I'm glad you know how to pronounce it. Mackin*aw*. Only tourists and outsiders say *nack*. You been here before? "

Taffy shook her head. "My mother used to come here when she was a little girl and she taught me to say it that way. I suppose you've been here? "

"Every summer," David said. "My grandmother has a house up near the cliff over to the right of the fort."

Taffy watched the island rise slowly from the water, high and beautiful, green-crowned and trimmed with the white lines of the fort. "Do you know where Sunset House is? "

"You mean that funny old hotel down near the shore road? "

Taffy didn't approve of his description. "It's a hotel," she said stiffly. "My mother owns it now. At least she probably will own it by the end of the summer."

"What happened to the bird woman? " David asked. "That Miss Irwin who owned the place? It was a regular hangout for gulls because she always put food out for them and for other birds. That's why we called her the bird woman. She was sort of batty about them, I guess."

"I don't know about that," Taffy confessed uneasily. "I only know that we're going to live there."

The ship was nearing the island, and passengers crowded the forward deck. Taffy waved excitedly to her mother, who put her book aside and joined her.

"This is David Marsh, mother," Taffy said. "David, this is my mother, Mrs. Saunders, and I guess I haven't told you my name. It's Taffy."

David made room for Mrs. Saunders at the rail and pointed toward the island. "That sort of white crescent along the water is the harbor," he told Taffy. "There's only a narrow beach there full of stones. The big beach is around the point to the left — that's where the Indians used to pitch their tents in the old days. Sunset House is at the right tip of the crescent, a big white house near the edge of the water."

"We'll go by it in a little while," Mrs. Saunders said. "Do you see that white building to the left of the fort — the one with columns across the front? That's the Grand Hotel. It's probably larger than all the fort buildings put together."

Taffy regarded the huge white building with a frown. She wasn't going to like anything more imposing than Sunset House. Then her attention swung back to the fort.

"Is it a real fort with soldiers and cannons?"

"It was a real fort," her mother said, "but it isn't garrisoned any more. The State of Michigan has taken it over to preserve it as a place of historic interest."

"Can you go inside? I mean behind the walls?"

"Sure," David answered. "I've been inside lots of times. If you want, I'll take you through it."

Taffy studied the fort's slanting white walls and square blockhouses. Her imagination was beginning to work and something exciting started to happen inside her. It was as though Mackinac promised mystery, adventure, something strange that had never happened to her before. It was as though the island were speaking to her across the water:

"*Along my beaches, in the shadow of my trees, behind my guarding walls, and at the end of my trails, something awaits you. Sometimes you will be afraid, but you will not turn away.*"

Her mother nudged her, laughing softly. "Taffy, David gave you an invitation." Her eyes twinkled. "Don't mind my funny daughter, David. She goes off in trances and nobody knows what's going on in her head. I think she's going to grow up to be a writer or a poet."

Taffy blinked away the vision. "I'd love to go through the fort," she told David.

He looked at her a bit queerly. "O. K. Either I'll come

down to the hotel and get you sometime or you can climb
the hill to my grandmother's house. Here — I'll draw you
a map to show you where it is."

With a stub of pencil and a borrowed scrap of paper he
drew a grubby sort of diagram. Taffy was not sure she understood the zigzagging lines, but there were names of
places and roads and that should help.

"It's easy to find," David assured her. "You can tell the
house gate by the ship's lantern hanging over it."

Mrs. Saunders touched Taffy's arm. "There's Sunset
House, that big old house with the turrets and cupolas and
the long stretch of green lawn coming down to the water."

Taffy searched until she picked out the turrets and cupolas. Down by the water's edge a small figure was seated
upon a rock. The boat wasn't close enough for Taffy to be
sure, but the figure looked like that of a girl. It was just
possible that Donna Tuckerman — if it was Donna Tuckerman — was going to turn out to be about her own age,
in which case the island would promise fun for the whole
summer. David was nice. But she was a little tired of all
the scrambling and climbing and running boys expected
you to do. It would be fine to have a girl living right in Sunset House whom she could have for a friend all summer.

She waved frantically at the small, seated figure. But
though she waved until the ship had moved into the crescent harbor and the rock was out of sight, the small figure
remained motionless and unresponsive.

Taffy felt her spirits fall. Probably it was her imagination
running away with her again, but she had a queer feeling
that there would be no warm welcome for the Saunders
family at Sunset House.

CHAPTER
❧ 2 ❧

Who Is Celeste?

TAFFY lost David in the crowd going down the gangplank to the dock, and did not see him again. Some vacationers, her mother had told her, spent a week or more on the island, but many simply took the lake cruise and were back on the boat before nightfall. These unlucky ones had only one hurried day to spend on Mackinac.

The lively activity of the dock filled Taffy with a tingle of excitement, and she shook off her disappointment over the girl who had not waved. Carriage boys with placards on their caps — college students, probably — were calling the names of their hotels. Taffy knew that no automobiles were allowed on the island and that transportation was by horse, by carriage, and by bicycle. Her quick eyes caught the words "SUNSET HOUSE" on the cap of a tall, lanky boy.

"I'm Mrs. Saunders," her mother told the boy in her gay voice.

It seemed to Taffy that a look of surprise crossed his face. And no wonder, she thought in resignation. In slacks, mother simply did *not* look like the owner of a hotel. But there was nothing she could do about that — absolutely nothing. The last time they'd seen daddy at the hospital — the day they'd gone to say good-by for the summer — he had pulled her close and whispered that she'd better "keep an eye on that mother of yours." This business of looking after mother was one of the jokes she and her father shared; but mother *did* have a way of blithely getting into the most complicated snarls.

Now she was talking to the hotel boy and handing him the baggage checks. " Will you get our suitcases now or come back for them later? "

" I'll put them on a pushcart now," said the boy, " and come back for them."

" Then perhaps we can get along to the hotel," mother said cheerfully.

He shook his head. " There's a couple more ladies should be on this boat." Passengers were still crossing the gangplank, and he lifted his voice: " Sunset House! Sunset House! "

" Oh-oh! " Mrs. Saunders said. " I'll bet — " She let the sentence trail off.

Taffy followed the direction of her gaze. Two grayhaired, elderly women were coming primly down the dock. One was tall and looked more severe than her companion.

" I'm afraid they're for us," mother whispered. " They're the kind Aunt Martha doted on. If I could give them a shock — "

" Oh, mother, don't! " Taffy pleaded. Maybe this was what her father had meant when he'd asked her to keep an eye on mother. " Maybe we need customers."

" Guests, honey, guests." Her mother was laughing. " I'm only joking, of course. But — " she broke off and Taffy wondered if she really was joking, " I'll bet we'll be sorry."

Running a hotel, Taffy decided, was going to be a big responsibility.

As mother had suspected, the two women were for Sunset House. The taller one looked at mother, at Taffy, at the carriage boy, and then back at Taffy.

" Are you *both* going to Sunset House? Miss Irwin never took children. There were never any about, except the housekeeper's little girl. And she is a quiet child and is never allowed to bring other children around."

Suddenly Taffy felt sorry for Donna Tuckerman. No wonder Donna, if it had been Donna, had not waved an arm off at the prospect of another girl's coming to the hotel.

"I'm Miss Irwin's niece, Elizabeth Saunders," mother said. "I'm taking over Sunset House for the summer. And this is my daughter, Taffy."

The tall woman looked, Taffy thought, as though she considered this very bad news indeed.

"Hattie, dear," she said to her companion, "this is Mrs. Saunders, the new manager at Sunset House."

Hattie said, "How do you do, Mrs. Saunders," and then looked at Taffy. "Hello," she said surprisingly, and Taffy caught what might have been a flash of a smile, though it disappeared so quickly she couldn't be sure.

"I am Miss Clara Twig," the tall woman went on, "and this is my sister, Harriet. Sister is delicate and needs the rest and quiet we always found at Sunset House. I hope everything there will continue unchanged."

"We will try to keep our guests happy," Mrs. Saunders said pleasantly.

The carriage boy led the way toward the street at the end of the dock, and all about them the morning sparkled with sunshine and activity. Down the middle of the thoroughfare ran a long row of carriages, two stamping, restless horses to each carriage.

Mrs. Saunders wrinkled her nose happily. "It hasn't changed a bit since I was here as a little girl. The island's always quiet until boat day and then it comes to life. You're going to love Mackinac, Taffy."

Taffy was loving it already. The hotel carriage had two rows of seats behind the driver. Moving quickly and not too politely, she managed to get the first of the two rear seats for herself and her mother. She would have liked to

be up beside the driver, whose name, she had discovered, was Sam.

"This is Main Street," mother said, as the carriage moved out into the stream of traffic, "and it really is Main Street. There are a few back streets up the hill, but all the shops are down here."

For a little while the clop-clop of the horses' hoofs on the road seemed the only sound on the island.

"Mrs. Tuckerman is well, I hope?" Mrs. Saunders asked, in an effort to make conversation.

"Not this morning," said Sam. "There was a little trouble, but I guess it's all right now."

Taffy wanted to ask, "What kind of trouble?" but her mother's look warned her in time. Apparently one shouldn't talk about trouble before guests.

However, Miss Clara Twig had overheard and was making little clucking sounds. "Mark my words, Hattie," she said, "it's Celeste. Martha Irwin was the only one who could handle her."

Taffy glanced at her mother. One of her mother's eyelids gave a quick, reassuring wink.

"There's the fort, Taffy," she said. "That statue in the park below the walls is Marquette. There's a wonderful sunset view of the Straits from up there on the cliff."

Taffy listened, and looked, and was interested; but somewhere at the back of her mind a name was repeating itself. Celeste! Who was Celeste? And what did it take to handle her? She wished she dared ask Sam, but she knew she shouldn't. But there were other questions she could ask.

"How old is Mrs. Tuckerman's daughter?"

Sam shrugged. "I can't say for sure, but I guess she'd be around twelve."

Taffy hugged herself. Just her age. She'd have a twelve-year-old girl for a friend. That girl on the rock probably hadn't been Donna.

Having made up her mind to that, Taffy settled down to enjoy the ride. The narrow, pebbled beach David had pointed out ran along the right of the road, its stones white in the sun. She would probably be able to wade there, and it looked as though there might be some good flat stones for skipping over the water. It seemed as though she had only begun to enjoy the motion of the carriage, so different from the motion of a car, when the ride was over and they were at Sunset House.

She scrambled out of the carriage and stood looking up at the building. The hotel was three stories high, with slanting roofs set at various angles and odd windows popping out here and there. Around the lower floor ran a wide, sleepy-looking veranda, hung with hammocks and furnished with rocking chairs.

Her mother had come up behind her. "Honey," she chuckled, "we're going to wake this place up."

Somehow Taffy wasn't sure that she wanted Sunset House to wake up. It looked right this way, sleepy and quiet. Houses had personalities of their own, just like people. To wake this place up, to set radios blaring and people rushing in and out, would be like putting the Twig ladies into slacks.

She went up the steps with her mother and into the hotel. Taffy had stayed at a good many hotels and she knew about lobbies and desks where you checked in and got the key to your room. But Sunset House had only a small hallway, softly carpeted. On one side double glass doors were closed on what was obviously the dining room. On the other side a wide doorway opened onto a room that was like a big living room, with the sort of old comfortable furniture you might see in a home — not hotel furniture at all. Opposite the door of the big room a graceful staircase curved toward the upper floors.

No one was in sight — not even a clerk behind a desk. Sam ushered in the Twigs and gave no sign that the empty hall surprised him.

" If you'll sit down for a minute in the lounge," he said, " I'll take Mrs. Saunders up to her room. Then I'll tell Mrs. Tuckerman that guests have arrived."

Miss Clara Twig's sniff seemed to say that things were certainly not being run as they had been in Miss Irwin's day. Sam led the way up the winding stairs. Mrs. Saunders followed him lightly and quickly, but Taffy's steps were slow.

Where was Donna Tuckerman? You'd have thought she'd be curious enough to be waiting on the front steps. That was where she'd have been, Taffy thought, as her hand moved upward along the polished rail. She was awfully tired of regular hotels; she knew she was going to like this one.

Sam and her mother had gone ahead to a third-floor room that opened at the end of the long hallway. Taffy wanted to move slowly, getting acquainted with the house inch by inch. She had a feeling that you couldn't dash up to this house and be friendly with it right away.

No, making friends with it was going to be a little like making friends with a dog. At first you'd just talk to it quietly until it began to trust you. Then you would put out your hand — just hold it out and not touch anything. And when it was sure that you really were a friend, the house would take you in. The walls would whisper their old, old secrets to you, and the doors would open and —

A door *had* opened behind her, very, very softly. She walked slowly along the carpet of the hallway and waited for footsteps to sound behind her. Why had the door-opening sound been so quiet? Why were there no footsteps?

Mother was talking to Sam. Taffy, reaching their door, turned quickly and looked behind her. She was just in time to catch a brief glimpse of dark eyes in a small brown face. Then a door at the end of the hall closed as quietly as it had opened.

Taffy turned and walked thoughtfully into the room she was to share with her mother during their stay at Sunset House.

The Gulls Cry

COME in, honey, and shut the door," Mrs. Saunders called, as Sam went off for Mrs. Tuckerman. "I'm glad they gave us this room. See if you can guess why."

Taffy took one last look down the hall, but the door at the far end still presented a blank, white surface. She closed her own door with a firm click and turned to look about the room. The wallpaper was an old-fashioned pattern — blue garlands of intertwined cornflowers. The furniture was old-fashioned too, but graceful and exactly right for this house.

Mother moved about, opening drawers and looking into the one closet. They couldn't unpack until Sam brought up their bags, but mother had an air of settling into the room.

"See this?" she said, moving to the bureau with a mirror above it as large as a lake. "The design on this crocheted mat divides right in the middle. We'll use it for our boundary. The right side is mine, and the left is yours. And we'll see who keeps whose side the neatest."

The idea of such a contest had no appeal for Taffy. She suspected she would not be the winner. She was trying to see why her mother was glad to have this particular room.

"If you'd just turn around," Mrs. Saunders said. "You haven't even looked in that corner."

Taffy turned and gave a little cry of pleasure. Part of

the room seemed to have changed its mind and decided to go off in a direction of its own, jutting into what was practically a separate room, with its own ceiling and window. The ceiling slanted overhead, and the window opened under a peak of roof, looking out over other sloping roofs that were part of the hotel.

From the window Taffy could see the hotel driveway and out over the tops of trees toward the hillside rising far above. There were houses up there, their roofs visible through the greenery. The room had two other windows, but neither was a special window like this one.

" Oh, mother! " Taffy cried. " Please, may I have this part of the room for mine? A table and chair would just fit it. It would be — oh, it would be practically a room of my own! "

" That's what I thought of when I saw we had this room," Mrs. Saunders said. " Once when I came on a visit Aunt Martha let me have it for my whole stay. I think I was about your age, and I can still remember how special it seemed to me."

It was odd, somehow, to think of mother as being twelve and living in this very room. Odd, but nice. It was a little like having a sister as well as a mother.

" I'd better go downstairs," Mrs. Saunders said. " It's about time for lunch. I wonder if they still ring that Chinese gong at mealtime."

Taffy followed her mother out of the room. As she hurried down the hall she noted that all the doors were tightly closed, as though the house did not trust her yet, as though it did not know her well enough to open its heart and take her in. Only one little bit of it was hers — a window and one corner of a room. But that was a start.

She heard voices and looked over the stair rail to the floor below. A tall, smiling, rather handsome woman was coming up the stairs to greet her mother.

" I'm Sarah Tuckerman," she said, holding out her hand.
" I'm sorry I wasn't at the door when you arrived."

Taffy decided the mother of the still invisible Donna
looked a little too dignified in spite of her smile. Her gray
hair was neatly done, and she wore a dark-blue dress with
spick-and-span white lace at the throat. Taffy wondered
what she thought of mother's slacks.

" I'm glad you're not ill," Mrs. Saunders said. " Sam
hinted that there'd been some sort of difficulty this morning and I was afraid — "

The smile left Mrs. Tuckerman's lips and she looked
worried. " Celeste's been seeing omens again. When that
happens we can't do much with her. She suddenly decided
not to lift a finger in the kitchen, and we're unprepared for
lunch. That's why I was occupied and didn't know you'd
arrived. I think your coming has upset her."

So Celeste was the cook! But why, Taffy wondered in
astonishment, should their coming upset her? And then
she saw mother's shoulders take on a resolute look. Daddy
always said mother was an " actionist" who, instead of
worrying, " upped and did something." Plainly, mother,
not yet ten minutes at Sunset House, was going to do
something now.

" What about lunch?" she asked.

" We'll have to serve sandwiches," Mrs. Tuckerman said.
" This is a small hotel and the same people, more or less,
come here year after year. In one of the large hotels on the
island sandwiches could be ruinous, but here there's a sort
of family air. They know Celeste and are familiar with her
moods, though, thank goodness, she doesn't often walk out
of the kitchen."

" How many are in the kitchen?" Mrs. Saunders asked.

" Four — Celeste, an assistant cook, and two girls to pre-
pare vegetables and clean up. Celeste dominates the
kitchen; when she goes on strike, the other three are nearly

helpless. They're making an ordeal of preparing sandwiches."

" We'll have to change that," Mrs. Saunders said, as
though preparing a hill of sandwiches for a small army of
hungry guests was something she took in her everyday
stride. " But I can't think why Celeste should be concerned
about me. I understand how much the success of the hotel
depends upon her. I'm certainly not going to interfere or
make changes."

" It — it isn't that — " Mrs. Tuckerman seemed reluctant
to go on.

As though both words and hesitation had escaped her,
Mrs. Saunders led the way down the stairs. On the last
step she paused and snapped her fingers. Taffy knew she
had been seized with one of her inspirations.

" I know! I'm going to tell the guests that Celeste has
temporarily deserted us. I'll invite any who wish to come
to the kitchen and make their own sandwiches, any kind
of sandwiches. They'll probably think it a lark."

Mrs. Tuckerman looked doubtful, but there was no
stopping mother once she got a big idea. She walked gaily
toward the lounge to make her announcement.

Taffy was on the last flight when Mrs. Tuckerman looked
up and saw her. The smile came back to the housekeeper's
face.

" Hello," she said. " You must be Taffy Saunders. Donna's
been looking forward to your coming. Would you like to
look at the garden before lunch? You can go out the rear
door over there."

Taffy started willingly toward the door. Some women
were talking on the rear porch. One of them looked up and
smiled as Taffy went down the steps. She wore slacks — so
mother had been right!

The garden was beautiful. A lawn, green and smooth,
stretched to the water's edge, so soft and inviting that Taffy

was tempted to roll across it. The flower beds made lovely
patterns of color against the green of the grass as they
curved about the edge of the lawn. There could be a kind
of happiness in just looking at something beautiful, Taffy
thought.

She wished she knew the names of the flowers. Living
in hotels so much one never got a chance to learn about
flowers. Someday, when the Saunderses had a house of
their own, she'd help mother plant a garden and she'd
know the name of every flower in it.

She dropped to her knees and buried her nose in a bed
of delicate, greenish-white blooms. Then she sat happily
back on her heels to look around at the garden and up at
the house. As she did so, a curtain moved at one of the
third-floor windows. Someone had been looking down at
her.

She considered the window soberly. Yes! It could match
the door that had opened and closed in the hall. The same
person who had peered at her in the hall and looked down
at her from the window was probably now watching her
from behind the curtain. It gave her a little prickle at the
back of her neck to be watched secretly.

She got up from her knees and went down to the rocks
at the water's edge. A strange stillness lay over the island.
Not that there weren't sounds, but they were individual
sounds. The faint, distant echo of horses' hoofs and carriage wheels; a church bell, deep and golden; waves lapping the rocks at her feet; the wild screaming of gulls out
over the water. City sounds shrieked at you in a mixed-up
roar. But here every sound was its own and somehow
seemed to add to the sense of quiet.

A voice, almost at her elbow, startled her. "What are
they saying?" it demanded. "Tell me! What are the birds
saying?"

Taffy turned quickly and for a moment could only stare.

A woman, half hidden by a bush, sat on a large rock not far away. She wore blue dungarees and a plaid shirt, teen-age style — though she certainly was not young — and on her bare feet were beautifully beaded Indian moccasins. Her black hair was wound in heavy braids about her head. Her skin was dark, and so were her eyes.

"The gulls," she insisted, ignoring Taffy's astonished stare. "What do they say?"

On the boat Taffy had thought the gulls sounded almost human. Now it seemed as though this time she *must* understand their cry if only to answer this strange, dark woman. As she held her breath, the cry of the gulls came to her more clearly. It *was* a word.

"Why," Taffy said, "it's as if they are calling over and over for help! I can hear it as clear as anything: 'Help! Help! Help!'"

The dark coronet of braids nodded. "Do you know what it means when the gulls cry for help?"

"No, I don't. Isn't that what they scream all the time?"

The woman sighed, as if discouraged by such ignorance. "It is only when they warn us that the gulls cry for help."

"Warn us? About what?" This was strange.

"Have you ever seen a storm on Mackinac?"

"No," said Taffy. "I only came here today." Sun danced on the bright blue water, and the summer clouds were harmless wisps in an almost clear sky. It certainly didn't look as if it were going to storm.

"You will see such a storm as only Mackinac can know," the woman said darkly. "It will bring bad luck. They expect me to cook for all those foolish ones who think only of their stomachs when such a storm is coming. Let them go hungry for a day. It will be good for them."

"They won't go hungry," Taffy explained. "My mother is inviting them out to the kitchen to make their own sandwiches."

For a moment the woman looked furious. Then the idea of Sunset House guests going out to the kitchen to make their own sandwiches seemed to strike her as funny. She burst into laughter that stopped as suddenly as it had begun. "You're the little girl, aren't you? Miss Irwin's great-niece?"

"And you," Taffy said politely, "must be Celeste. They said you were seeing omens. What do you see when you see omens?"

Celeste's eyes took on a deeper darkness. "I've told you — it is the warning of the gulls. They are right — these people who say they can do nothing with me. But they can't do without me either. This sandwich thing — it will not last. They come to Sunset House because the cooking of Celeste Cloutier is as famous as the cooking of the other Celeste, her mother, in the great days of the Cannon."

Taffy could make no sense of her words, so she said nothing.

After a moment Celeste went on: "Today is boat day. That means many extra guests for my cooking. Ha! Sandwiches. Ham and pickle and cheese. They will go away and never come back."

"I don't think that's very nice," Taffy said indignantly. "If it went on, the hotel might have to close."

"You are very smart to see that," Celeste said, as though pleased.

The cook, plainly, was not in sympathy with the fortunes of the Saunders family. Taffy wanted to ask why her mother's coming had been disturbing, but this didn't seem to be the right time. Besides, there was something else she wanted to know. Not that she couldn't guess the answer, but she wanted to make sure.

"There's been someone watching from a window on the third floor," she said.

Celeste turned her head. "You mean the second win-

dow from the right? That will be Donna. She is curious
about you. Poor little one! "

Donna certainly chose an odd way of showing her interest, Taffy thought. Well, she couldn't hide forever behind doors and curtains. The mouse would have to come
out of her hole. But there was still one more thing Taffy
wanted to know.

She searched her pocket, brought out the paper on
which David Marsh had drawn a map, and smoothed it as
best she could. " Can you tell me how to find this place? "

Celeste frowned over the sketch.

" Now I see it! " she exclaimed. " This will be easy to
find. Across the shore road by the hotel there is another
road going uphill. It is bad walking because it is steep and
stony. When you get to the top, take the road to the right.
It will wind, but do not leave it. It will bring you to this
house you want to find."

" Does it take long? " Taffy asked.

"Twenty minutes perhaps. There is a short cut at the top of the hill, but you do not want to take that."

"Why not?"

"Before sundown it would be safe. After that — no."

"You mean it's dangerous? Steep or something?"

Celeste watched a gull go flapping by close to shore. "It is a goblin wood," she said. "To take the shorter way you must cut through the goblin wood."

Taffy felt a tingle of interest. "What is a goblin wood?"

Suddenly Celeste was impatient. "Children!" she cried. "Always asking questions. Always bothering. Go and see for yourself. But do not say I did not warn you. Now then, run away and play. Quickly! I wish to think."

At that moment a deep-voiced musical gong sounded from the hotel, the echoes dying away on a long, drawn-out note.

So lunch, Taffy thought, some sort of lunch, was being served. And they still used the Chinese gong! Well, she was hungry and anything at all would taste good. She started across the lawn and Celeste's brooding voice followed her:

"Sandwiches! Ha! Sandwiches at Sunset House!"

CHAPTER
❧ 4 ❧
The Goblin Wood

A SMILING Mrs. Tuckerman, from whom all worry had disappeared, met guests at the door of the dining room and escorted them to their tables. The change, Taffy suspected, was mother's doing. Mother was so sure about everything she did that she often made other people feel safe and sure too. Daddy said the kind of spirit mother had was catching and that it did other people good to catch it.

The tables in the dining room were filling rapidly. A dignified gentleman, whom Taffy had heard Mrs. Tuckerman call "Mr. Gage," chuckled as he took a sandwich from a platter.

"A bologna masterpiece, my dear," he said to his wife. "I suppose Celeste would be shocked, but I like bologna sandwiches."

Mrs. Gage didn't seem quite so pleased as her husband.

Mother's scheme really was working, Taffy thought as she stood beside the dining-room door. At least, it had worked this time. As she stepped aside to let a guest by, her elbow touched something that gave out a faint hum and she saw that she was beside the Chinese gong. The black wooden stand from which it hung was carved with scaly, bulging-eyed dragons. The gong itself was big and round and flat. Made of bronze, probably. Taffy remembered reading about Chinese gongs in a book from the library. The mallet hung on a hook at the side of the frame. The stick was made of bamboo, the head thickly padded.

Perhaps sometime mother would let her ring the gong.

Mrs. Tuckerman touched her elbow. "I'll show you to your table, Taffy. This is where Donna and I sit. Your mother thought it would be nice if you joined us. She's eating in the kitchen today, but usually she'll sit here too. Donna should be along any minute."

The housekeeper went back to her place at the dining-room door, and Taffy looked about the pleasantly bustling room. It certainly seemed as though Sunset House was doing a good business. There was scarcely an empty table, and waitresses in neat blue uniforms and frilly aprons moved in and out of the kitchen, bearing trays of sandwiches and hot and cold drinks. They looked as if mother was making it fun for them in the kitchen.

She liked the room, Taffy decided. The walls were of pine paneling, which gave it a woodsy sort of look that fitted in with Mackinac. Between pictures of island scenes hung snowshoes, skis, and Indian articles. On the wall directly above her head was a curious sort of stick, with a small gaudily painted clay head at one end. While she was wondering what it was, a young waitress brought her a glass of water.

"Hello, Taffy," the girl said, smiling. "Your mother told me about you. My name is Doris."

Taffy liked her at once. She had lived in hotels enough to know that an unpleasant waiter or waitress could spoil a meal, so it was nice to have a girl like this waiting on their table.

"How would you like a tomato and lettuce sandwich with mayonnaise and a pickle?" Doris asked.

Taffy giggled. Doris hadn't thought that up all by herself; she'd been told by mother. It was a standing joke in the Saunders family that Taffy would take a lettuce and tomato sandwich (with mayonnaise and a pickle) no matter what was on the menu.

As Doris went off, Taffy saw a girl coming across the room. She was small and dark, and her hair was cut short and ruffled in soft curls. It was the kind of hair straight-locked Taffy had always longed for in her dreams. The girl's skin was tanned, but there were no freckles to disturb its clearness.

"Hello," Taffy said. "Are you Donna?"

The girl nodded. For a moment her dark eyes examined Taffy gravely and then looked away as she slipped quietly into the chair across the table. The silence lasted until Doris brought Taffy's sandwich and a glass of milk.

"Are you two getting acquainted?" the waitress asked. "You ought to have fun this summer. I wish I had time to run all over the island with you."

Taffy and Donna exchanged solemn looks, and then, surprisingly, they both smiled at the same instant. Donna's nose wrinkled and a dimple showed in one cheek.

"I saw you on the rocks this morning," Taffy said. "I waved and waved from the boat."

"I — wasn't sure it was you," Donna told her. "And anyway —" She didn't go on to explain about "anyway." The word hung between them with nothing to follow it up.

Taffy bit into her sandwich and concentrated on preventing mayonnaise from oozing out of the corners. Donna was hard to talk to, yet she didn't seem exactly unfriendly. Taffy tried again.

"I should think it would get lonesome without other girls to play with. Didn't Aunt Martha ever allow children to stay here?"

"I guess she didn't like children much. She said children ran about and shouted and broke things. Will your mother let people with children come here?"

"Of course," said Taffy, not knowing anything about it, but feeling on fairly safe ground. "Mother likes children."

Donna considered that soberly. She seemed undecided

about something and not quite able to make up her mind. Then she flashed her swift, surprising smile.

" I'm glad you've come. I make up games and I have lots of fun by myself. But sometimes games need two, instead of always just one."

After that there were no uncomfortable stretches of silence. Taffy felt reassured. Probably Donna was shy, more than anything else. They'd get along all right as soon as they had time to get acquainted.

Doris brought Donna a sandwich, and Taffy thought about plans for the afternoon. Right after lunch she would see if she could find David's house. David had promised to show her the fort, so maybe they could arrange to go through it tomorrow. Besides, she wanted to have a look at what Celeste had called the " goblin wood." She wasn't in the least worried about its being a frightening place. Maybe it would be a little spooky, but that would be fun.

" What's a goblin wood? " she asked abruptly.

Donna looked startled.

" Celeste says there's one at the top of the hill."

" Oh, Celeste! " Donna shrugged. " She likes to make up crazy things like that. She's lived on Mackinac all her life, and her family lived here from the beginning — you know, from the time of the fur traders. Her head's full of Indian stories about spirits on the island. She's partly French, and I think she had an Indian great-grandmother."

" Anyway," Taffy said boldly, " I think I'll go up the hill this afternoon and have a look at this wood she was talking about. I'm not afraid of Indian spirits."

Donna's dark eyes rested on her in a way that was curiously thoughtful. " Maybe you'd better not say that too loud. Celeste says the island spirits are everywhere, even in this hotel."

Taffy glanced around quickly, as if she might catch an Indian spirit wandering through the dining room. Her eyes fell again upon the curious club on the wall.

"What's that?" she asked.

Donna looked at the paint-streaked clay face. "It's an Indian war club somebody found in one of the caves on the island."

All at once Mackinac seemed very close to Indian times, and Taffy found it hard to remember that no longer ago than yesterday she had been in a modern city like Chicago. The island had no automobiles, and up the hillside ran the walls of an old fort. Here at the hotel was an odd French-Indian woman out of the past, and on the walls were snow-shoes and an Indian war club. And on the cliff high above Sunset House was something Celeste called a goblin wood.

"Would you like to come along?" she asked Donna. "I'm going to look for the house of a boy I met on the boat."

For a second the other girl wore that curiously thought-ful look. "I can't. I have to practice."

"On the piano?" Taffy asked.

"No — dancing. I always practice for a while in the afternoon."

Taffy felt a little envious. "I used to take dancing les-sons, but I wasn't any good at it. Do you like it?"

Donna glowed. "I love it! I love it more than anything else in the world! Someday I'm going to be a great dancer. I won't be stopped by anything. Not by anything." All in a moment she had become solemn.

Taffy, startled by the intense words, felt like saying: "Well, don't look at *me*. I'm not trying to stop you." But it didn't make sense that Donna should think she was.

What an odd girl! Shy one minute, friendly the next, and then sort of hostile. It was as if Donna were mixed up about something and not able to make up her mind. Well, if she didn't want to climb the hill, she needn't.

As Taffy crossed the dining room the Twig ladies were

at a small table by a window. Miss Clara Twig did not see her, but Miss Hattie looked up and once more gave her a quick half-smile.

Out in the hall Mrs. Tuckerman was talking to a round, bald, genial little man. This time the housekeeper was not smiling, but she had the same dark-browed look Donna had been wearing a moment before. Taffy found herself thinking how much Mrs. Tuckerman and her daughter resembled each other.

"I'm sorry, but we haven't a vacant room," Mrs. Tuckerman said. "Not one."

"I'm delighted to hear that Sunset House is doing so well," the man said warmly. "Of course, I'm not surprised. Good management means few vacancies."

Mrs. Tuckerman turned a bright pink, and Taffy was surprised at how much it became her. She looked younger and a little flustered.

"Surely," the man went on, "every table in the dining room is not taken as well. I have been dreaming of Celeste's cooking for weeks."

"It won't be Celeste's cooking," Mrs. Tuckerman told him. "It will be sandwiches."

He didn't seem surprised by the news. "That sounds as if Celeste had gone on another strike."

Without answering, Mrs. Tuckerman led the way to a table. When she came back to her post by the door, she was still flushed.

Then she did what Taffy thought was a surprising thing. She left the door and peered into the old-fashioned oval mirror at the foot of the stairs. She gave her hair one or two quick pats and smiled at her own reflection. It was not at all, Taffy realized, the kind of polite smile she had worn before.

At that moment she caught Taffy's interested gaze upon her in the glass and her smile vanished. "Did you have a good lunch?" she asked. Then, without waiting for an answer, she said: "A hotel is a dull place for a little girl. Why don't you go outside in the fresh air?"

Taffy was bewildered by the change she had witnessed. "I want to ask mother something first. Do you know where she is?"

"I think she's still in the kitchen. If you go out the back way, you won't have to go through the dining room."

Taffy followed directions and found the kitchen. Surely it was the biggest kitchen in the world, and the most sparkling. There were all kinds of cupboards, and dozens of shining pots and pans hung in orderly fashion above a huge stove.

The kitchen girls were still making sandwiches, and several waitresses were arranging them on plates. They were all laughing and talking. Supervising the scene was Mrs. Saunders, and it was quite evident to Taffy that her mother was having a good time.

She'd tied up her hair in a blue bandanna and she had a streak of mayonnaise on her chin and an alarmingly long butcher knife in one hand. Every now and then she waved the knife in the manner of a baton, and Taffy feared she'd cut off a passing waitress's ear. Somebody had wrapped her into an apron that must have belonged to Celeste, for it went around her a couple of times.

But mother in this new role was not the most surprising thing to be seen in the kitchen. Over in a corner, out of the path of the waitresses and out of reach of mother's waving knife, Celeste was perched on a stepladder, her knees drawn up and her moccasins hooked about the top rung. She was eating a very large sandwich.

Mrs. Saunders saluted Taffy with the knife. "Hi, honey! Everything all right?"

"Everything's fine," Taffy said. "Will it be O. K. if I go

up the hill and look for David's house? I know the way. Celeste showed me."

Mother looked doubtful, and for a moment Taffy thought she was going to refuse. Then she said: " All right. But don't stay away too long this first time."

" I won't," Taffy promised quickly, and got herself out of the kitchen before her mother could go into detail about how long was too long.

It was shorter to cut through the hallway of the hotel than to go around the house outside. She hurried through the screen door, barely avoided a collision with Miss Clara Twig, and dashed out the front door at the very moment the rear door slammed. She had a glimpse of Mrs. Tuckerman's reproving look and then she was outside, running across the road.

Oh, dear! She hadn't meant to run into Miss Twig and she hadn't thought about the door slamming. Why did things like this always happen to her?

The road uphill was steep and stony, as Celeste had warned her. Taffy decided that, in spite of burs, the grassy bank along the road's edge made for better going. But she'd better remember to pull the stickers out of her socks before mother went to wash them.

At the top of the hill she took the road to the right. This was a better road, a winding road, and the walking was good. Houses were scattered along the way, some closed and neglected, others open and bright with fresh paint.

The road left the houses behind and ran across a little bridge. Taffy found her heart beating more quickly. Was she getting near the goblin wood? Where was the short cut?

The road dipped downward over a little hill and there the short cut was. She recognized it without the slightest doubt, for there was the goblin wood, a forest of tall pine trees, strange and dark and forbidding. Through the trees she could see the rise of a hill that cut off light and added to the gloom. The pines rose straight and high, but every tree was dying and all the lower branches stuck out starkly bare of needles.

It was only a dying forest, Taffy told herself. Of course she would walk through it.

Her feet sank into a springy pine carpet under the trees. The trunks were black and the shadows gloomy. What if she couldn't get out? What if she walked and walked and there was no way out, no way back? What if this wood were enchanted? Bright sunshine, houses and people, were distant, out-of-sight things that belonged to another world. She had better walk quickly and get away from here.

She took three quick steps — and stopped. Without a sound a boy had stepped out from behind a tree. He was rather a tall boy, with the dark skin of an Indian. He wore blue overalls and a red shirt, and there was a certain dignity about him.

" H-h-hello," she faltered.

The boy did not answer, but stared at her steadily.

The skin began to creep at the back of her neck. " If I w-w-walk this way, will I come to the road on the other side? "

The boy did not answer, and his eyes did not waver. Only his blue overalls saved her from panic. Goblins did not wear overalls and red shirts.

Something crackled faintly behind her and she whirled about. The sound had been made by a scurrying chipmunk. She turned toward the Indian boy again and could scarcely believe her eyes. He had vanished as silently as he had appeared.

She hurried to the tree where she had seen him, but there was no one hiding in the shadow of its trunk. He had to be somewhere; the ground hadn't swallowed him. Probably he was still watching her from some new hiding place.

Suddenly the one thing she wanted was to get out of this wood. She ran, and the rusty needles were slippery beneath her feet. Beyond the gloom of the strange trees she saw a strip of road winding away, and welcome sunlight. In another moment she had left darkness behind.

She kept running until she came to a fence with a gate in it, and a ship's lantern above the gate. The gate was unlatched, and, still running, she went down the walk to the front door of David's home.

CHAPTER

❧ 5 ❧

The Lost Key

TAFFY pressed the button and heard a bell sound inside the house. In a moment or two a gray-haired woman opened the door.

"Something tells me you're the young lady my grandson met on the ship. Isn't your name Taffy? I'm Mrs. Marsh. You'd better come in while I call David. Have you been running? You're flushed and out of breath."

"Yes, I have," Taffy said. She could not tell this bright-eyed old lady about her fright. Already it was beginning to seem like a dream — except that she knew it wasn't a dream. There *had* been a boy in the goblin wood — an Indian boy — and he had not liked her.

Mrs. Marsh walked to the foot of the stairs and called up them. "Da-vid! Oh, Da-a-vid! Taffy's here to see you."

David came downstairs in the galumphing way of a boy. "Hi-ya!" he called. "Come on up and see the tower room. I'll let you look through grandfather's binoculars if you're careful not to drop them."

It would be easy to pick up her friendship with David. The stairway ran up three flights and then turned into a steep ladder with rubber treads and a brass handrail — like the ladder to the officer's section of a ship. David reached down and pulled her up the last few steps. "This is the quarter-deck," he explained.

The tower room was built to resemble the cabin of a ship. The windows were portholes, and all sorts of mysterious seagoing objects decorated the walls.

" My grandfather used to be a lake-boat captain," David said. " When he retired, he fixed this place up so he could feel at home and always see the lake."

Taffy went to one of the round windows. The view was wonderful. She could see a corner of the fort and the little pebbled beach of the harbor. And she could see far out across the water, past the little island with the lighthouse on its point and the bigger wooded island on the left, clear to the blue line of the Michigan shore — the mainland. Down in the Straits a freighter puffed along lazily.

" Goodness! " Taffy cried. " I can see for miles."

" Look through these." David handed her the binoculars and showed her how to adjust them.

The pebbled beach came up so close that she felt she could reach out a toe and touch it. She moved the glasses slowly to the left and then gave a triumphant squeal.

" There's Sunset House. I can see it as clear as anything."

The big white house filled the lenses. She picked out the gables and the windows and the sloping roofs. Up on top of the main roof was a sort of railed platform.

" I wonder what that is? " Taffy said, and turned the glasses over to David.

" That's what they call a widow's walk," David told her. " In the old sailing days captains' wives used to have places like that on their houses, where they could go up and watch for their husbands' ships. There's probably a trap door that leads to it from somewhere inside."

He gave Taffy the glasses, and she moved them about until they brought into view her own private window in the room she shared with her mother. She turned to David in sudden excitement.

" You know what? I could hang signals in my window.

I mean, I could if I had important news to tell you some-time."

"What sort of signals?" David wanted to know.

Taffy's lively imagination went to work. "We'll have to figure out a code. Red for danger, of course. And white if all's well."

Surprisingly, the practical David entered into the spirit of the adventure. "And yellow for 'Yes' and blue for 'No.' And —"

"Yipes!" Taffy cried. The glasses had moved away from the window and picked up the side garden of Sunset House. Donna was standing on the veranda talking to a boy in the yard — a boy who wore blue overalls and a red shirt.

Her mother hated to hear her say, "Yipes!" but some-times she just had to say something strong. It was so sur-prising to see Donna talking to the very Indian boy who had frightened her!

"That's the boy I saw in the goblin wood," she told David excitedly.

David looked bewildered. "What *are* you talking about?"

"S-s-sh!" Taffy said.

There was no reason, of course, to think it meant any-thing that the boy in the woods was now talking to Donna Tuckerman, but seeing them together made her uneasy. She remembered Donna's lapse into coldness as they were finishing lunch and the unfriendliness of the Indian boy. She wished there were binoculars that brought in sound as well as image. As she continued to peer through the glasses, the boy disappeared around the corner of the house and Donna went inside.

"What are you looking at?" David demanded. "Let me see!"

Taffy turned from the window. "There's nothing more to see."

"Well, creepers!" David said. "You don't have to be so mysterious."

"Creepers" — that was a good word. Maybe mother would prefer it to "Yipes." But she'd better satisfy David's curiosity before he became too impatient. She needed someone with whom she could talk over the things that had happened since she came to the island.

She started at the beginning, with Donna's refusing to wave to her, and ended with the goblin wood and the strange Indian boy who had just been talking to Donna. She told about Celeste's moods and omens, and about how important it was that her mother run the hotel successfully this summer so that the Saunderses could buy a home.

David listened with satisfying interest. "I guess this *is* a mystery," he said when she had finished.

Taffy hadn't looked at it quite like that. When there was a mystery, you got busy and looked for the reasons behind what happened. Then everything turned out fine; the good people won out and the bad people were punished. Of course, she and her mother were the good people; only there didn't seem to be any bad people — just people who were a little puzzling.

"It's just like your mother said," David told her, laughing. "You go off in a trance and don't hear anything anybody says. We ought to plan a campaign."

"What kind of campaign?"

"Well, a — a course of action."

"But *what?*"

"Oh, we'll figure something out! Maybe we could start by having a look at that wood. Maybe we'd find a clue."

That seemed like a good idea. Besides, though Taffy would never have admitted this to David, now she wouldn't have to walk through the wood alone. Even though she knew the Indian boy had gone down the hill, she felt uneasy about meeting him again. She said good-by to Mrs. Marsh, and set off willingly with David.

It was just as well, she thought, that she was starting for the hotel. Already it was probably what mother would call "too long."

David boldly pushed his way through the stark branches.

"I come this way all the time," he said. "I never thought it was especially spooky. I guess girls get scared easily."

Taffy followed him indignantly. One of the things she had liked about David was that he didn't say belittling things about girls and try to act he-man. Now he was spoiling it.

"It was somewhere around here," Taffy said stiffly. "But I don't see what clues there'd be. You can't leave footprints on pine needles, can you?"

David examined the bark of a tree and studied the ground. Probably, Taffy thought, he was showing off the way boys did.

Then he straightened and looked at her. "You know what I think? I think probably that Indian was walking through the wood just like you, or me, or anybody and didn't mean to scare you. The cook had you thinking about creepy things, so when you saw him all of a sudden you were ready to be scared. Then you imagined he was looking at you as if he didn't like you. And when he went away you thought he hid."

David looked very pleased with himself at this deduction, and Taffy could only feel annoyed and helpless. *She* knew what she had experienced in this wood. But she knew too that when a boy came to his own conclusions there wasn't much you could do about it.

Then something white against a tree trunk caught her

eye. She reached past David and snatched loose a sheet of paper wedged under a slash of bark.

" So I just imagined everything, did I? " she demanded triumphantly. "Well, then, Mr. Know-It-All, listen to this." She kept him waiting for a moment to punish him and then read aloud: "Why don't you go back where you came from? We don't want you on Mackinac. You make the manito angry."

David took the paper from her. " See! " he said. " I knew we'd find a clue."

Taffy started to sputter and then saw he was only teasing her.

" I guess I wasn't so smart after all," he admitted, and she liked him better right away. Lots of boys would never admit they were wrong.

"After all," she said generously, " it *was* your idea to come back here. I'd never have come alone."

He was studying the paper again. " I wonder what this picture of an animal's head is at the end? "

Taffy wasn't sure. " It looks a little like a dog's head."

" I don't think so. The nose is too pointed. Could be a fox, maybe. But I wonder why? "

Taffy was concerned with another problem. "Why doesn't he want me here? I'm sure it's meant for me. And what is a manito? "

" That's an Indian god — one of the spirits they used to believe in. He's just trying to scare you."

Taffy fought down an apprehensive shiver. She wasn't, she told herself stoutly, in the least afraid of Indian spirits — not with David there beside her. " Do you want to go through the fort tomorrow? That's what I came to find out. I forgot to ask mother, but I'm sure she'll let me go."

David brightened as an idea struck him. " I know! Let's try out our signal system. Yellow's for ' Yes.' If you can go, hang something yellow in your window."

Taffy agreed, and he turned back at the edge of the wood. She hurried down the road and, when she reached the hotel, found her mother picking flowers in the garden. A basket rested on the grass, and mother's scissors were going clip-clip in time to her gay humming.

"We're going to have flowers on every table tonight," her mother said. "And do you know what?"

"What?" Taffy asked. She could see that mother was off on one of what daddy called her "steam-engine" trips.

"I'm going to be hostess tonight."

"Oh, mother, that's swell!"

"I'm taking some of the work off Mrs. Tuckerman's shoulders. This is something I thought I might learn easily, though at first I probably shan't do it as well as she does. She has a very nice hostess manner and she's tactful about handling the guests."

Taffy remembered one guest Mrs. Tuckerman had not handled very well — the pleasant bald man who had wanted a room.

"You'll be heaps better," she told her mother stanchly. "And prettier too."

Mrs. Saunders made her a bow. "Thank you kindly. But I'm afraid you're prejudiced. Anyway, I *would* like to put some life into this place. Sometimes it depresses me."

Taffy looked up at Sunset House, drowsy in the afternoon sun. Sleepiness, she was sure, suited it. Maybe it wouldn't be happy if they woke it up too much. Of course, if waking it up meant flowers and someone pretty and smiling to show the guests to their tables —

"Wear your blue dress, mother," she pleaded. "And pin your hair up high the way daddy likes it. Then I'll write to him tomorrow and tell him just how you looked and what a success you're being as a manager."

Her mother wrinkled her nose, but Taffy could tell she was pleased.

"There's something I haven't told you," Mrs. Saunders continued. "Something about Donna."

"Donna? What about Donna?"

Mother went back to her flowers. "These blue ones are delphiniums, honey. They'll look nice on the tables, don't you think? Delphiniums and ferns."

"Mother, do stop being exasper-maddening!" Taffy pleaded. "Exasper-maddening" was one of daddy's words.

Mrs. Saunders smiled. "Donna's quite a dancer. Her mother wants her to train seriously for ballet. So I suggested to Mrs. Tuckerman that we have an entertainment tonight for the guests. Doris plays the piano and can do her accompaniment. Mrs. Tuckerman was pleased, I think. Anyway, Donna is going to dance."

For a second Taffy felt a little envious. All she had done at dancing school was to get her feet tangled up and irritate the teacher, or else forget what she was supposed to be doing with her feet because of the interesting things that went on inside her head. If only she could dance with her thoughts! But thoughts didn't show to anybody else. She threw off the brief moment of wishing for other girls' talents. It would be fun to have an entertainment.

"It seems," mother went on, "that Aunt Martha didn't approve of Donna's dancing. Doris tells me she quarreled about it last year with Mrs. Tuckerman."

It seemed to Taffy that she could hear again the intense way Donna had said that nothing was going to stop her from becoming a dancer. Perhaps Donna had thought mother would be against her dancing. Then tonight ought to make Donna and Mrs. Tuckerman both feel better.

"But what if there isn't any dinner, mother?" Taffy asked anxiously.

Mrs. Saunders laid a sheaf of blossoms in her basket. "Are you thinking of sandwiches? That happened because Celeste threw her tantrum at the last minute. The assistant cook could take over if necessary, though I'm afraid the guests could tell the difference. But I've found a way to make Celeste happy."

Taffy laughed softly. " You do manage things! "

" Celeste's a musician at cooking — an artist. So I'm going to send to Chicago for some special delicacies she wants. She's very pleased, and I don't think we'll have any more trouble."

Taffy sighed her relief. " Now I know everything's going to work out all right. And we've got every room filled."

Mrs. Saunders looked up from her flowers. " I wish we had, honey, but there are still two vacancies." She scrambled to her feet, blew Taffy a little kiss, and was off for the house on a run.

Taffy frowned. Two rooms vacant? But how queer! She had heard Mrs. Tuckerman telling that smiling little man there wasn't a vacancy. Why was she turning business away when mother needed it? A new mystery was added to the others. This was getting to be like a jigsaw puzzle. She followed the path to the back steps, deep in thought. Right when you believed everything was going to be fine, some new piece of the puzzle jumped askew and refused to fit in.

Several people were reading in the lounge. They paid no attention to her as she looked around to see if she might find a clue. After all, David had found one when she hadn't believed he would, so why couldn't she? But there were no clues in sight. She wondered idly about the door on the other side of the lounge. It couldn't be a private room, since there were no bedrooms downstairs. She crossed the room to investigate, turned the knob, and let herself through the doorway.

The small room in which she found herself proved to be nothing more exciting than an office. This must have been where Aunt Martha did her bookkeeping. There was a big old-fashioned desk, with a high back filled with empty pigeonholes, and before it a swivel chair with a leather pad on the seat. Against one wall was a table piled with neatly tied stacks of old magazines.

Old magazines were always interesting. Taffy moved one of the stacks and a small cloud of dust sifted upward, making her sneeze. Maybe she'd better not disturb these without permission. Grownups didn't like it when you stirred orderly things into an interesting state of confusion.

Her gaze, moving about the office, was caught by a picture hanging on the wall. It was the strangest picture she had ever seen. She was sure it hadn't been painted by a very good artist, though she recognized the scene. Those were the rocks at the water's edge in front of the hotel, and, in the distance, the little island and its lighthouse. The water was much too blue and the waves didn't look real. But the most surprising thing of all was the figure seated on the rocks.

It was a woman in a long flowing dress with birds all around her. The birds were not even as real-looking as stuffed birds she had seen, but she could tell what they were meant to be. One big fellow was perched on the woman's shoulder. Judging by his silver-gray color, he was supposed to be a gull. In the corner of the odd picture were the initials " J.B."

Whoever " J.B." was, he or she must have been a friend of Aunt Martha's. Because, of course, the portrait was of Aunt Martha. It fitted in with what David had called her on the boat — the "bird woman."

Taffy turned away from the picture and continued her examination of the room. Now she saw still another closed door opposite the door through which she had come in. She walked over to it and turned the knob. She turned it right and left and tried pushing, but nothing happened. The door was locked.

"You're not supposed to go in there!" said a voice behind her.

Taffy turned quickly. Donna Tuckerman stood in the open doorway that led from the lounge.

"You can't go in there," she repeated. "*She* wouldn't like it."

"Who wouldn't like it?" Taffy asked.

Donna nodded in the direction of the picture. "Miss Irwin. She never allowed people to go into that room unless she was with them."

"But Aunt Martha isn't here any more," Taffy answered.

Donna tilted her curly head to one side as though considering this. "Anyway you can't go in. The door's locked."

"We can get the key."

Donna gave her an odd smile. "Nobody knows who has the key. It's been lost since Miss Irwin died. Nobody's ever going to open that door." She turned and went out of the room, leaving an uneasy, puzzled Taffy to stare after her.

Slowly Taffy's bewilderment turned to frowning concentration. Why had Donna boasted that the door would never be opened? What was in the room that had to be hidden behind a locked door?

She tried the door again. The room's windows opened on the veranda, so perhaps there was a way in by means of the windows. She would have to see. Here was a real mystery — a locked room and a lost key! Something hidden away that Aunt Martha wanted no one to see.

Wait until David heard this!

CHAPTER
⊱ 6 ⊰
Treasure or Secret

TAFFY hurried through the lounge, tripped over Mr. Gage's outstretched feet, and saved herself by catching at a small reading table. The table and the lamp on it rocked, but fortunately nothing crashed.

"Careful, young lady," Mr. Gage smiled.

Taffy could feel her cheeks growing pink. Why *did* she do things like that?

She went on to the veranda, forcing herself to walk sedately. The shades on the windows of the locked room were drawn so she could not see in, and she could not reach high enough to push the windows up. A stick might help. She leaned over the rail, searching for something suitable, and was startled to see the Indian boy in blue overalls and red shirt watching her from the grass.

This time she recovered from her surprise more quickly. "Why," she demanded, "did you leave that note for me up in the woods?"

He looked at her for a moment with his steady gaze. Then, without a word, he walked out of sight around the house. Taffy did not mean to let him go so easily. She ran down the steps and around the corner of the house, but he had disappeared again and the side yard was empty.

There was nothing to do but give up the chase. As she turned back to the house, she saw a length of wood lying near the foundation of the veranda. That ought to serve her purpose. But though she pushed against the frames with all her strength, she could not move any of the windows. Like the door, they too were locked.

She entered the house and went straight to the dining room. It was time her mother heard about these mysteries.

Mrs. Saunders was at a table near a window, arranging flowers in a vase.

"Mother" — Taffy was breathless — "there's a big, locked room on the other side of the house and all the windows that open on the veranda are locked too!"

Her mother took the news calmly. "Mrs. Tuckerman says the key is missing."

"But what's in the room? Why did Aunt Martha lock it?"

"I don't know why. When I was here years ago, it was a library full of old books. Not very interesting books either. I know because I tried to read some of them. It was never locked in those days."

"How are you going to get the door open?"

Mrs. Saunders stood back to admire the effect of a delphinium-fern combination. "How does it look, Taffy? Do you think it needs a bit more green?"

"It's all right." Taffy scarcely looked at the vase. "But what about the locked room?"

Mrs. Saunders took up another spray of fern and added it experimentally to the vase. "I'll get a locksmith out here one of these days. I almost hate to open it because it means clearing out a lot of old rubbish. There are many more important things to be done around here before we get to that."

Taffy did not agree, but she remembered what her father said sometimes when mother behaved in what he called an "exasper-maddening" way. He said the minute you tried to push, she'd balk. If Taffy pushed about the

room, mother might take it into her head not to open it all
summer. She abandoned the subject regretfully.

"Mother, have you seen an Indian boy around here?"

"There are quite a few Indians on the island, honey.
An Indian boy works here at the hotel, taking care of the
yard and doing odd jobs. I think his name is Henry."

So! No wonder the boy knew Donna.

"I don't like him," Taffy said with conviction. "He
doesn't want us here."

"Nonsense!" mother said cheerfully. "Why should you
think that?"

"He wrote a note and fastened it to a tree where I'd
find it. Look!" Taffy took the sheet of paper from her
pocket.

Mrs. Saunders read it and smiled. "That's a nice touch
about the manito. But how do you know this was meant
for you?"

Taffy explained what had happened in the goblin wood,
but Mrs. Saunders was unimpressed.

"You can't be sure it was intended for you. The note
might have been there all along and you only saw it when
you came back. Don't worry — it's probably some childish
prank."

Taffy put the note back into her pocket. She wasn't
through yet.

"There are other things. I think Celeste wants to hurt
the hotel, and Donna acts funny. Why don't *they* want us
here?"

Mrs. Saunders put her flowers down soberly. "Perhaps
we'd better have a little talk, Taffy. Trying to see that
everything goes right at this hotel is a big job. I think you
know how important it is that I do it well. There isn't anything I want more in the world than to settle down in one
little house; that's the only reason I'm willing to leave
daddy for this whole summer."

Taffy nodded. *She* wanted that house too. Maybe she wanted it more than either mother or daddy.

"So you have to help me as much as possible. You mustn't make things difficult by being unfriendly and — "

"But I *haven't* been unfriendly!" Taffy objected.

"Donna seems to feel that you're unfriendly."

Indignation left Taffy almost speechless. "Did Donna tell you that?"

"Her mother told me. Well, actually she didn't tell me. But I got the impression — "

"But it isn't true! It isn't fair! It's Donna who sometimes acts unfriendly."

Mrs. Saunders waved a calming finger at her. "Don't get excited about it, honey. You have to remember that Donna has lived here alone a lot. She's not used to other girls. You'll have to give her a little time to get to like you."

Taffy stared at her toes and felt unjustly treated.

Mrs. Saunders put a finger under Taffy's chin and tilted her head. "You have to remember that you are a very imaginative young lady. You'll have twice as much fun in your life as people who lack imagination and you'll see more than they do in the world around you. But sometimes, honey, your imagination may lead you into seeing what isn't there."

Taffy pulled her chin away. "You just don't understand!"

"Perhaps I do. Perhaps Mrs. Tuckerman has been worried about our coming here, because it might affect her position as housekeeper. Her husband died when Donna was very young and she has had to work hard. She wants Donna to have opportunities and that isn't always easy. You have to see *their* side." She put an arm around Taffy's shoulders and gave her a little squeeze.

Taffy walked solemnly toward the door. Then she remembered something and turned back. "Will it be all right if I go to the fort with David tomorrow? "

" Of course," her mother said, and Taffy went upstairs to hunt for her yellow sweater.

Maybe, she thought as she fastened a line of string across the window and draped the sweater over it, she hadn't tried hard enough to make friends with Donna. Maybe if you came to understand why another person behaved in an odd way, you'd be more patient. A warm, pleasant glow began to spread through her. It was good to feel generous and kindly toward the world. Next time she saw Henry she'd even smile at him, and she'd be so nice to Donna that the other girl would have to respond.

But there still remained the problem of the locked room. That had nothing to do with kindness and generosity. No matter what mother said, people didn't put a lot of old books in a room and then lock it up. Rooms were locked for important reasons.

You might lock a room to hide a treasure that was valuable to you, or because there was something you didn't want touched by other people. Or you might lock a room to hide a secret. But then you didn't go out and lose the key. You hid it carefully. Or perhaps someone might have stolen it —

Taffy shook her head so violently that her braids swung back and forth across her shoulders. Oh, dear! Here she was doing just what her mother had warned her not to do. She was letting her imagination run off with her.

The room was locked and someone must know where the key was. Someone must also know what the room contained. Who would be more likely to know than Celeste?

She was tempted to dash downstairs at once and ask the cook. But Celeste would be in the kitchen preparing dinner. What the cook could tell her would have to wait until after Donna had danced.

Taffy looked toward David's house. She could see the

tower room sticking up through the treetops; somebody might be waving to her from the window. She waved back with enthusiasm, knowing that if David were looking through the glasses, he could see her plainly. She wished they had thought up a signal that would mean "mystery deepens"; the danger signal wouldn't exactly do. A locked room didn't necessarily mean danger.

Dinner that night was a pleasant affair. Mrs. Saunders had put on the blue dress and had pinned up her hair. Taffy felt secretly proud as she watched her mother greeting guests with just the right touch of friendliness. The flowers looked lovely on the tables, and the food that came steaming in from the kitchen was delicious.

Taffy had no opportunity to try her new plan of friendliness, for neither Donna nor Mrs. Tuckerman came to dinner. Doris said Mrs. Tuckerman did not think Donna should eat just before she danced, so they were going to wait.

The tables were well filled tonight. People from other hotels and from private homes often came to Sunset House for Celeste's cooking. Though Taffy looked about for him, she did not see the round little man whom Mrs. Tuckerman had turned away earlier in the day. For some reason she felt sorry. He had looked as if he'd be fun to know.

Doris was jumpy and nervous. "I'm always this way when I have to play," she told Taffy as she took away her soup plate and brought a plate of fish so handsomely arranged that you could practically wear it for a hat.

Taffy whispered a question before Doris could go off again. "Do you know what's in the locked room?" she asked.

"I didn't know there was a locked room," Doris told her and went to wait on the next table.

Probably, Taffy reflected, Doris didn't bother about the rest of the house, or know too much about it. Probably

Doris was old enough to mind her own business — something Taffy was sure she herself was not. Minding one's own business the way grownups were always instructing her to do could be very dull indeed. Now Celeste would probably mind someone else's business with as much interest as her own. Taffy began to be impatient for the evening to get on and the dancing to be over so she could find her chance to talk to the cook.

CHAPTER
❧ 7 ❧

Donna Dances

SOME of the extra dinner guests stayed for the dancing. The middle of the lounge floor had been cleared and chairs were lined up around the walls and across one end.

Taffy, ushering, was busily engaged in seeing that every-one found a seat. Most of the regular Sunset House guests knew Donna and seemed to like the idea of seeing her dance. But there was one dissenting voice.

" Poor Martha! " Taffy heard Miss Clara say. " She would never have permitted this. After all, that child's dancing was what caused all the trouble."

Miss Harriet, as usual, said nothing, but Taffy thought her eyes looked bright and interested.

Doris had changed from her uniform to a sweater and skirt and had put in her hair a blue flower from one of the tables. The wide door to the lounge was open, and Taffy found a perch halfway up the stairs which gave her a special sort of box seat. Donna and Mrs. Tuckerman were using a screened corner of the dining room for a dressing room, and now and then she caught a glimpse of Donna's white ballet costume.

Just before the entertainment began, Celeste came to a window that opened on the veranda and seated herself on its ledge. She had changed her dungarees for a summery green dress with puffed sleeves, and her thick black braids had been freshly plaited. They gave her head the crowned look of a queen. Taffy found herself wondering what the cook thought of all this. Her face was like a mask guarding her thoughts, but it seemed to Taffy that it wore a waiting look. Maybe it was one of her omens she was waiting for.

The piano rippled into something gay and lilting, and Donna ran out of her "dressing room" and onto the "stage." She was a different Donna tonight. Her eyes danced and her smile was the radiant smile of someone doing what she loved to do more than anything else in the world. She was so graceful, so enchanting, that Taffy found a lump of emotion in her throat. Sometimes a sight that was especially lovely made her want to cry — as though there was a pleasant sadness about beauty.

Then the gay little interlude was over and everyone was applauding. Taffy clapped as hard as she could. When she paused, because her hands were stinging, she heard continued applause behind her. She turned quickly and saw that the Indian boy had seated himself on the stairs just above her. Under this new, happy spell Taffy could not regard him as mysterious or unfriendly.

"Donna's good, isn't she?" she asked, smiling.

Henry looked down at her with his odd, sharp gaze. "She's very good," he said quietly and looked back at Donna.

He's her friend, Taffy thought, and for an instant wished he could be her own friend too. In spite of the way he had scared her, she had a feeling that he would be worth knowing, and that David would also like him. Perhaps, after this dance of Donna's, they could all be friends.

Donna began her encore, and when that was over Mrs. Saunders said there would be a short intermission while Donna changed her costume for a couple of tap numbers. Taffy wished Donna wouldn't. She'd never cared much for tap dancing. It was showy, clattery stuff, not magically beautiful like ballet. She'd have liked the other dancing to go on forever.

However, Donna brought even to tap an elfin sort of loveliness. Her costume was bright raspberry, ruffled with tiers of silver, and she looked as pretty as she had looked in her white ballet skirt. She was good at tap too. Taffy, remembering her own helpless effort to learn a simple routine, knew just how good she was.

She looked over at Celeste, but there was no change in the cook's expression.

She's still waiting, Taffy thought. Waiting for something that hasn't happened yet.

Once more Donna bowed to the applause, and once more the clapping hands demanded that she dance again. She glanced at Doris, and Doris smiled back. The waitress had got over her nervousness.

Merry music set Donna's feet tapping gaily, never missing a beat, working into a complicated routine. Taffy glanced back to see how Henry was enjoying this part of the dancing, and at that moment there was a crash and the sound of breaking glass. Doris faltered in the middle of a measure and then went on, but as Mrs. Tuckerman walked quickly across the lounge to open the door of Miss Irwin's office, Donna stopped dancing.

Taffy stood up on the stairs as Mrs. Tuckerman flicked on the office light. The picture of Martha Irwin lay face up on the floor, glass shattered by the fall. From where she stood, Taffy could see a painted Aunt Martha, surrounded by painted birds staring up through the shattered wedges of glass.

Mrs. Saunders took charge of matters cheerfully. "A picture was jarred from the wall," she told the guests. "Let's continue our interesting show."

But Mrs. Tuckerman remained where she was, looking down at the broken glass. Into the awkward pause came Miss Clara Twig's audible voice.

"If I believed in such things," she said, "I'd think Martha herself had put a stop to this. In fact, I'm half inclined to think it anyway. The dancing should never have been permitted."

Mrs. Saunders walked to the piano and spoke to Doris. The little waitress picked up the music where she had left off and Donna, after a doubtful look at her mother, went on with her dance. Taffy suspected that the falling picture had upset Mrs. Tuckerman badly, and Donna must have been upset too, because the life went out of her dancing.

The person in whom Taffy was most interested had disappeared. Taffy slipped down the stairs and out the rear door to the veranda. It was getting dark and the Mackinac night was sharp. She ought to go for a sweater, but then Celeste might get away.

As she ran across the lawn toward the water's edge she flung up her arms in the darkness, partly to warm herself and partly because out here where nobody could see she could pretend that she was as graceful and lovely as Donna and that the bright stars were the eyes of an audience.

A shadowy figure was seated on the rocks. Taffy let the stars go back to being stars and set her feet into their usual earth-bound steps. Celeste did not look at her.

"You were waiting for the picture to fall, weren't you?" Taffy asked.

"I did not think the dancing would be allowed to pass," Celeste said slowly.

Taffy seated herself on the rocks. "Didn't you like Donna's dancing?"

"It was beautiful. But if *they* do not like it, who am I to set myself against their will?"

"Whose will? What do you mean?"

Celeste shook her head. "Some things must never be named. When you name them, you open the way."

Taffy tried to see her face in the gloom. She felt a little awed by the cook's manner and words. Was Celeste playing a sort of make-believe game of her own? Anyway, there was a question she had come here to ask.

"Celeste," she said, "why did Aunt Martha keep that room locked all the time?"

"To keep out the curious, naturally."

Taffy tried again. "But what's in it that she wanted to keep the curious away from?"

"What else but her friends?"

"*What* friends?" Taffy was becoming impatient with all this mystery.

"Those who were her dearest friends." Celeste's arms moved in a dramatic arc above her head, taking in sky, water, and island. "Those that are not out there. Those they brought to her. It is a good thing the door is locked. They must never be allowed to get out."

If only, Taffy thought, she could pin Celeste down to one simple, sensible answer. "But where is the key?" she asked.

"Gone," said Celeste. "No one will ever find it."

" How do you know? Did Aunt Martha tell you? Did she lose it? "

" Certainly not. She was not a careless person at all. *I* lost it. I took it from among her keys after she was gone, and I lost it very well."

Taffy listened to the night sounds of wind in the trees and waves against the shore. After a while she spoke gently as if to a child.

" Could you find it again, Celeste? "

The woman shrugged. " Only the Cannon knows the secret."

The Cannon! That was the second time Celeste had spoken of the Cannon. What had she said before? Something about the " days of the Cannon." Something about the other Celeste who was her mother. That hadn't made sense either.

" Come, you must not mind me," Celeste said unexpectedly. " I have lived so long on this island I sometimes think I am a part of it like the great Arch Rock, or the pebbles on the beach, or the trees on the heights."

Taffy sat very still.

" Michilimackinac! " Celeste rolled the syllables on her tongue. " That is the old Indian name. Some say it means ' Turtle's Back,' because the island looks like a turtle rising from the water. Others say it means ' Home of the Great Spirits.' No matter — it is older than all beginnings. First the manito. Then the red man. Then the French and British and Americans. Battles have been fought on island meadows, and secret landings made in the night. Flags have been furled and unfurled."

Taffy held her breath. When Celeste talked in this grand way, it was like listening to something out of a book.

" In the old days there was the great fur trade, when the *voyageurs* came through the Straits in their canoes and Mackinaw boats to land on the beaches and bring the island to life with laughter and song. All through the winter they stayed in faraway woods to trap their furs. Then, with the breaking of the ice, they came to Mackinac to be paid by the fur company. Those are the people I come from. That is the time when I should have lived."

"It sounds wonderful," Taffy said in a small voice.

Celeste began to sing softly. The words were French, and Taffy could not understand them, but the song had a throbbing beat. The waves and the wind in the treetops seemed to hold their breath and listen.

"They have not heard that song for a long time," Celeste said sadly. "John Jacob Astor moved his fur company on to the Northwest. The British gave the fort back to the Americans from whom they had taken it, and all the soldiers went away. There were no more *voyageurs* with feathers in their caps, riding their Mackinaw boats through the Straits. Now we have hotels and tourists and timid people who come only in the summertime. And Celeste Cloutier works as a cook at Sunset House."

Taffy could see that all this must seem very sad. The great days were gone. But the island still seemed an exciting place, and she wished there was some way in which she could comfort Celeste.

The silence lingered and presently her teeth began to chatter.

"You are cold," Celeste said. "Run back to the house quickly."

Taffy stood up and flapped her arms up and down, but she did not turn toward the house at once. "You said it was going to storm."

"I said that — yes. It will come. Tomorrow, perhaps."

Taffy looked up at the sky. There was no use in pointing out the bright, unclouded stars to Celeste. Once more she tried the subject of the locked room.

"What good did it do to lose the key? As soon as my

mother wants to open it she can get a locksmith."

"There will be a delay," Celeste answered. "And the longer we wait the better."

"But why? Won't the room be the same whenever it is opened?"

"Give them time," Celeste said, "and they will go to sleep. Asleep they can do no harm. That is why I lost the key — to give them time. But they are not asleep yet. Did you hear the rustling when the picture fell?"

"All I heard was a c-c-crash." Taffy's teeth were really chattering.

"Quick!" Celeste cried. "Into the house with you. Quick!"

Taffy gave up and ran across the lawn to the back steps. Once out of the raw wind her teeth ceased to chatter. Her mother came out of the lounge just then and saw her.

"Taffy! Where on earth have you been? I've looked everywhere."

"I was down by the water talking to Celeste," Taffy said.

Mrs. Saunders shook her head. "Outside without a sweater on? You have to remember that the island can get cold at night and in the early morning. Honey, what do you think? Some of the people who came to dinner tonight decided to spend their vacation here. Our two extra rooms are rented and the hotel is full!"

Taffy gave her mother a hug. "I'll bet they liked the flowers on the tables and you for hostess."

"Such flattery!" But her mother's laughter had a warm sound. "Time for bed now. Better run along." And then, as Taffy started upstairs, "Do tell me why you hung a clothesline up in your window and draped a sweater over it."

"That was a signal for David," Taffy explained. "It means I can go to the fort tomorrow."

" Oh! Well, if you think he's seen it by now, suppose you take it down. It doesn't look too well from the front of the hotel."

Taffy went upstairs. Maybe it would be better to arrange a special hour with David for signals. She might really need him one of these times if the mysteries kept growing. So far, there were just odd, unconnected questions that no one would answer.

CHAPTER

❧ 8 ❦

Meeting at the Cannon

IN THE morning, white fog blew in wisps across the garden and rolled in puffballs down the driveway. Trees and bushes were hazy green outlines that kept fading quietly out of sight.

Taffy, eating breakfast, watched the dining-room windows. Would the fog make any difference in the trip to the fort she and David had planned? Was Celeste's promised storm on its way?

She asked Doris, but the waitress shook her head. "Celeste will mutter about storms until one really blows up. Of course there always is a storm if you wait long enough. Celeste should have gone in the movies. I bet she'd be wonderful in a mystery thriller."

A few moments later Donna appeared and sat down in her place opposite Taffy.

"Hello," Taffy said, remembering that she was going to be extra friendly to Donna. "I liked your dancing last night. I wish I could dance like that."

The dimple came into Donna's cheek as she smiled. "Miss Irwin didn't like me to dance. She told mother —" But what it was that Miss Irwin had said, Taffy wasn't to hear, because Mrs. Tuckerman joined them at the table.

The housekeeper said, "Good morning," as though she did not find it a particularly good morning. "I have a headache," she explained, and ordered a cup of black coffee. " Did you like the entertainment last night? " she asked Taffy.

" I think everyone did," Taffy told her. " I hope Donna will dance again."

Mrs. Tuckerman was uncertain. " I'm not altogether sure — "

" Oh, mother! " Donna broke in. " Miss Irwin isn't here any more, and Mrs. Saunders likes dancing."

Mrs. Tuckerman was still unconvinced. " Everything is so unsettled — "

" You mean the place might go to the birds, after all? " Donna asked.

Mrs. Tuckerman shook her head at her daughter. It was the kind of warning, Taffy recognized, that mothers gave when daughters talked too much. But what an odd thing to say! She'd heard of going to the dogs, but not of going to the birds. And how could Sunset House be given to birds? Here was another touch of mystery!

Then David appeared at the dining-room door, so Taffy hurried the remainder of her breakfast. She had put on a pull-over sweater, not trusting the island to be warm. The minute mother said: " Good-by. Have fun and come back in time for lunch," she and David were off.

" Oh, I like this! " Taffy cried, fanning at a wisp of fog.

" It'll burn off after a while," David said. " If you look up you can see it's getting brighter. That's the sun trying to break through."

They followed the shore road through the soft, weaving fog. Now and then a house swam into view, only to be swallowed up again as soon as they passed it. Taffy told David that the Indian boy's name was Henry, that he worked at Sunset House and was Donna's friend. She kept the locked room, the lost key, and Celeste's reference to a Cannon that knew the secret of the key until last.

"There's a cannon up at the fort near the old block-houses," David said. "Maybe she hid the key there, though it sounds like a silly sort of hiding place."

The fog thinned away, and Taffy saw patches of water. The heights on the right with the fort upon them were still invisible, but this was where they could start to climb. Once the statue of Father Marquette looked down out of the fog, only to disappear almost at once.

"We'll take the road below the wall," David said, "and go in through the south sally port."

Suddenly, as they climbed, they came out into the bright sunlight of a Mackinac morning. Taffy could not suppress a squeal of pleasure. There was no land or water, only an island in the clouds, and she was on it.

"You'd better save your breath," David said practically. "It's a steep climb."

The white stone wall rose above them. They reached the sally port and walked into the fort. All about were neat, low buildings — barracks where the soldiers had lived and the quarters of the officers.

David led the way toward the blockhouse. Taffy had never before been in a place that gave her a sense of walking the same paths people had walked more than a hundred and fifty years before, when America was new. The blockhouse had a dank, musty smell. David went ahead, up a steep wooden ladder that led to the overhanging upper room. All around were loopholes through which guns could be fired. Taffy looked out toward the harbor through one of the deep-set windows and felt that she was back in the past.

Surely there would be wigwams on the sandy beach around the point, and, if she listened, she would hear the *voyageurs* singing in the village! If she looked, she would see them strutting about with cocks' feathers in their hats. And John Jacob Astor's men would be there, buying furs

to make beautiful the ladies of Quebec and Montreal and
Paris and London.

"Hey!" David cried. "Snap back to earth, will you?"

Taffy blinked the vision out of her eyes. "Goodness!
Were you talking to me? I was thinking of the *voyageurs*
Celeste told me about. Why did they wear feathers in their
hats?"

"They had to earn their feathers," David said. "I read
about it in one of grandfather's books. Only the head of an
outfit could wear a feather. But, look, I was asking you
about the will."

"I'm sorry," Taffy apologized. "What will?"

"The will your great-aunt left. Suppose your mother
doesn't get the hotel? Then who does? What happens to
it?"

Taffy shook her head. "We don't know. Aunt Martha
made that part of the will secret. There's a sealed envelope
that isn't to be opened until summer is over."

"But can't you guess? Haven't you any idea?"

"Mother said Aunt Martha did such queer things in the
last years of her life that there was no use trying to guess.
But Donna said something funny this morning at breakfast about the hotel going to the birds. Her mother hushed
her up. What do you suppose she meant about the birds?"

David was puzzled. "That doesn't make much sense. I
don't see how birds could come and live in it. Anyway,
how about looking at the cannon to see if that's where
Celeste hid the key to the locked room?"

They scrambled back down the ladder and out of the
blockhouse, past a stretch of stockade. On the grass beyond stood an old artillery piece, its muzzle pointed toward the harbor. But though they looked in every possible
crack and niche, there was no key. In fact, there was no
convenient hiding place for one. Anything thrust into the
cannon's muzzle could be easily seen.

"If this cannon knows any secrets, it's sure hiding them," David grumbled.

"I guess it could tell us plenty if it could talk," said a voice behind them.

Taffy, who had put her eye to the muzzle, looked up and recognized the round little man who had asked Mrs. Tuckerman for a room.

"Hello," she said, feeling that she knew him. "I'm sorry you couldn't get a room yesterday."

He looked surprised, and then smiled in recognition. "Oh, you're the young lady I noticed at the hotel. Maybe you're Mrs. Saunders' daughter, eh?"

It was Taffy's turn to be surprised. How could this man know her mother's name and that she had a daughter? But he had turned cheerfully to David.

"And who are you, young man?"

"I'm David Marsh, sir."

The man nodded. "Mrs. Thomas Marsh's grandson, perhaps?"

"That's right," David answered. "Do you know my grandmother?"

"Not well," the little man said, "but I've met her at social affairs. My name is Bogardus — Jeremiah Bogardus."

He was so friendly and cheerful that Taffy and David found it easy to accept him as one of their party. After that the three of them went through the fort together. One of the buildings had been made into a museum. Indian relics and weapons, articles used by the fur traders and the *voyageurs*, things left by the French and British during their occupation of Michigan territory were arranged in glass cases. After what was to Taffy a rapt hour, Mr. Bogardus glanced at his watch.

"Breakfast is well behind us," he announced cheerfully, "and lunch is well ahead. What would you two say to going down to the village for a bit of refreshment?"

That seemed a wonderful idea. They went downhill the quickest way and walked toward Main Street. It was quieter than it had been yesterday, with horses and carriages standing in a sleepy line. This was not a boat day, and vacationers staying on the island strolled the streets with a look of belonging. Probably, Taffy thought, they had learned to say "Mackinaw" by now, instead of "Mackinack," and considered themselves old-timers.

Seated at a table in a drugstore, she took her time over the menu, and Mr. Bogardus, unlike mother, made no effort to hurry her. Taffy considered reading a menu almost as nice as the final savoring of the selection she made. In her imagination she took a little taste of everything. Mother never understood that part. She always said, "Honey, you know you'll end up by having a black cow, so why don't you just order it to begin with?"

This time it took Taffy at least five minutes to "taste" everything on the list, so that when she finally told the waitress she wanted a black cow, she felt she was really getting what the menu had to offer.

"I must come down to Sunset House to see your mother," Mr. Bogardus said, when the orders had been placed before them. "After all, I haven't been in the hotel business most of my life without learning a little about it. I might be able to offer some useful advice."

Taffy looked at him with new interest. "You mean you've run hotels yourself?"

"In the Orient," Mr. Bogardus said, looking dreamy. "There was a little place out in Manila that did a good business with people from home. And there was a more ambitious hotel I managed in Hankow, China."

David's eyes widened at the mention of Manila and China, but Taffy was more interested in the hotels.

"Did they belong to you?" she asked.

"I'm sorry to say they didn't. I was a young man working for others. But it is still my ambition to own a hotel myself."

Taffy spooned rich vanilla ice cream out of her root beer and let it melt luxuriously on her tongue. She couldn't imagine anybody liking hotels enough to want to live in one forever. Even though this summer on Mackinac was going to be fun, it was the little house it would give the Saunderses that counted most with her.

Every time she thought about the house the picture in her mind came a little clearer. She'd like her room done in blue, she had decided. Blue was her favorite color, and it would be nice to have everything match. Oh, there'd have to be contrast, of course! Mother always talked about contrast when she was trimming things. Yellow, maybe. She could have a shade for her reading lamp with yellow and blue flowers on it. And she liked those flower pictures she had seen in stores — large sprays of flowers that came in pairs. Two of those on the wall above her bed —

She caught David's eye just then and came back from her dream world in time to hear the word "bicycle."

"I can ride a bicycle," she said quickly. "Someday when we get our own house my father says I can have one."

"You can rent one here," David said. "I've got one for the whole summer; they give you a special rate for that long a time. If you get one, we can take some real trips. Walking's too slow."

Mr. Bogardus suggested that they stop at the bicycle place near the dock on the way home. But when they finished their sodas and went outside, people were scurrying along with their heads bent against a rising wind. Signs rattled and flapped, and anything unattached was blowing down the street.

"There's going to be a storm," Mr. Bogardus said, "and it looks like a bad one. I'll see if I can get a driver to take you to the hotel."

The arrangement was quickly made. David and Taffy climbed into the seat and the horses clop-clopped away.

"Celeste told us there'd be a storm," Taffy said uneasily. "She said it would be a terrible storm and that it would bring bad luck to Sunset House."

David was unimpressed. "A storm's a storm. So what?"

"Look at the gulls!" Taffy cried, pointing.

Straight above their heads flew a dozen or more sea gulls screaming their cry of "Help! Help! Help!" It seemed to Taffy they were in a panicky sort of haste, as though trying to escape from the path of the storm.

The carriage came into the open on the road above the white stone beach. Wind tossed the horses' manes, spray blew over them, and out beyond Round Island ominous black clouds boiled into big thunder packs. Lightning slashed the sky in a zigzag, and Taffy heard the roll of thunder drums.

"It *is* going to be a bad storm," she said, and felt uneasiness tingle down her spine.

CHAPTER

⊁ 9 ⊱

Wings in the Storm

LUNCHEON was, Taffy thought, the nicest luncheon they'd had since coming to Sunset House. That was surprising because mother, escorting a guest to a table, had caught her eye and had cast a tragic glance toward the kitchen. But if the approaching storm had aroused Celeste to one of her omen moods, the mood had not been dark enough to send her from her beloved pots and pans.

For a while it looked as if the storm might miss the island after all. But the wind changed direction and black thunderheads began to roll toward it.

Taffy heard the wind thrashing treetops against the slanting roof of the hotel. Going up to her room, she hung a white slip in the window as an "all's well" signal for David — since all was still well. The day was growing dark as night, and she was afraid David would not be able to see the signal even with glasses. She could barely distinguish the bushes that bent over before the gale, looking like crouched women with their hair streaming in the wind.

She could no longer hear the gulls above the high moan of the wind, and the old uneasiness returned as she knelt on a chair by the window and put her nose against the glass. Then, even as she watched, the storm swept down upon the island. The big house shuddered and rain slashed the windowpanes. The garden disappeared in stormy darkness, then flashed to vivid life as lightning struck nearby. Taffy drew back from the window, blinded by the flash, her ears ringing from the crash of thunder.

She wondered where Donna was. Could the roof blow off? The way the wind was tearing at the house that seemed a possibility. Lightning flashed again and a broken tree branch flew by the window, just grazing the glass.

Taffy had had enough of being alone. She opened the bedroom door to find the hallway without light. At the far end a gleam marked the stairway, reflecting lights from the lower floor. She felt along the wall for the switch to light the upper hall, but as she clicked the switch a bulb glimmered and went out. At the same moment the glow from the stairway vanished. A wire had gone down somewhere and Sunset House was without electricity.

Taffy felt her way back to the room, found a flashlight, and hurried toward the stairs, picking out the way in the beam of the light. She wanted to find her mother. She wasn't frightened — of course not. But she didn't want to be alone in all this crashing and buffeting and blowing. Even though it was the last thing she wanted to think of, Celeste's prophecy of bad luck kept coming into her mind.

As she reached the first stair landing she heard a tremendous slap of wind against the house, followed by a crash and a thud. For a second Sunset House seemed to hold its breath. Then somebody began screaming in one of the rooms along the upper hall. Taffy stopped her plunge down the stairs and, scarcely conscious of what she was doing, ran back to the upper floor. There was no time to think of being afraid.

Without stopping to knock, she pushed open a door and the beam of her flashlight picked out a scene of confusion.

A window had blown in and something loose was flying about the room. Miss Clara Twig was still screaming. Taffy's light picked out little Miss Hattie, seated in the

middle of her bed, white and shaken, but not uttering a sound.

"Do something," Miss Clara cried hysterically. "Oh, this is terrible, terrible! A huge rock blew in and broke the glass. The entire building will go next."

Taffy heard steps racing up the stairs and knew that welcome help was on the way.

"It wasn't a rock," Miss Hattie said in a trembling voice. "It was something alive. It's under the bed."

Then dozens of people seemed to crowd into the room. Taffy saw her mother come through the door, a lighted storm lantern in her hand, her dress whipping about her in the wind. Behind were Mrs. Tuckerman and Celeste and Donna.

Taffy dropped to her knees and turned the beam of her light under the bed. Something fluttered and rustled and uttered queer little sounds that could scarcely be heard in the uproar.

"It's a sea gull!" she cried. "It's a little one, and I think it's hurt."

Miss Hattie slipped off the bed and knelt beside her. "I knew what came through the window was alive. Oh, the poor thing! Can't we do something about it?"

A little fearfully, Taffy stretched out her hand, but the sea gull took fright and fluttered against the wall, out of reach. She straightened up on her knees and looked around. Her mother was giving directions about boarding up the window temporarily, and Sam, the boy who drove the carriage, was on his way out of the room to get the boards.

Then Taffy saw Celeste standing in the doorway. In the wavering light of the lantern she looked mysterious and strange.

"There's a bird under the bed!" Taffy called to her. "That's what broke the glass. It's hurt and frightened."

Celeste came toward her. " If it is a gull — " Alarm was in her voice.

" It is a gull," Taffy told her. " A baby sea gull."

She refocused the beam of her flashlight, and Celeste peered under the bed. But she made no effort to reach the bird. When she stood up, alarm and satisfaction were mingled in her expression.

" This is what I knew would come. They will be angry now. There is serious trouble ahead."

" Who will be angry? " Miss Hattie asked gently. " What do you mean? "

Celeste only shook her head.

" She said the storm would bring trouble," Taffy explained. " She says the manitos told her."

Mrs. Tuckerman joined them beside the bed. When she saw the gull fluttering weakly in the beam of Taffy's light, she gave a cry of dismay.

" Throw it outside quickly. Get it out of the house."

Celeste put a hand on her arm. " Do not touch it. It is hurt. It must not die here."

" But what are we going to do about it? It can't stay."

Celeste said: " I will get Henry Fox. Henry will take care of it."

Even in the excitement of the moment Taffy caught the name Celeste had spoken. Henry — *Fox*. A fox's head had been signed to the note. So the Indian boy *had* written it.

" I think the storm is dying down a little," Mrs. Saunders said briskly. " Suppose we leave this room to be set to rights."

Miss Clara Twig had recovered to some extent from her fright.

" Come, dear," she said to her sister. " I think it's safer downstairs. Our nap is spoiled for this afternoon. As soon as it is possible, we will leave this place."

Miss Hattie turned to Taffy and spoke in a whisper. " I

hate naps," she said, and followed the older Miss Twig meekly downstairs.

Taffy looked after them worriedly. Mother would have to change Miss Clara's mind somehow. It would be bad for the hotel if guests started leaving. She got down on her knees again and looked under the bed.

A soft voice beside her said: "Poor little baby. I hope Henry comes quickly."

It was Donna — a gentle Donna, interested only in the bird.

"Will Henry know what to do?" Taffy asked.

"Indians know all about birds and animals. He especially likes the sick ones he can help to make well. I guess that's because he wants to be a doctor when he grows up."

Taffy was surprised. None of this fitted the surly, unfriendly picture she had formed of Henry Fox.

Behind her Mrs. Tuckerman said: "It's under the bed, Henry. Do something about it quickly. If only Miss Irwin were here! She understood gulls."

"I'll hold the light," Taffy offered as Henry crawled under the bed on his stomach.

He did not reach for the bird at once, but spoke to it in words Taffy could not understand. They were Indian words, probably. The bird stopped its terrified flutter. When he took it into his hands, it rested quietly in his grasp.

Very carefully he drew it out from under the bed and nestled it against him. Sam came in with boards for the broken window, and Mrs. Tuckerman started to help one of the maids straighten up and to sweep out the glass.

Donna hurried off and came back through the hall with two lighted candles in tall brass candlesticks. Henry seated himself on the top step of the stairs and examined the sea gull with gentle fingers. Watching him with the bird, Taffy thought, you had to like him no matter how he had behaved before.

"The young ones aren't very smart," he said. "An old one would know better than to be caught by the wind like that. This one hasn't lived long enough to be wise."

There was some magic in his hands that the bird seemed to recognize and trust.

"Is it hurt very much?" Taffy asked anxiously.

Henry shook his head. "I think it was just stunned. Nothing seems to be broken. When the storm's over, we can let it go."

"I wish we could keep it," Donna said wistfully. "I've never had a pet."

Taffy felt a quick, sympathetic understanding. "I've never had one either. We've always had to move around so much. When we get a place of our own, my father says I can have a dog."

"You're lucky," Donna said. "Mother can't let me have a pet because it might bother the guests. Once I had a turtle, but it died."

"They always die," Taffy agreed gloomily. "Having my own room and a pet is why I want a house more than anything. Oh, I *do* hope Miss Clara won't be so upset about the gull that she'll move out of the hotel!"

Henry was more interested in the gull than in the Twigs. "We ought to make a nest for it till we can let it go," he said.

Taffy jumped up from her place on the step. "I'll get something," she offered recklessly. "Wait here."

The storm was breaking a little and the hallway was not so dark. Rain still pounded on every slanting roof, but the thrashing of the trees had lessened. When she reached the room, Taffy looked about helplessly. Why had she promised to find something the bird could nest in? She and her mother had brought to the island only what they needed. Donna had lived here for years and would probably have a whole stock of boxes and baskets that might do. But somehow the nest had seemed a quick way to win Henry Fox's approval.

On the shelf in the closet was the cardboard hatbox that contained her mother's best hat. It was, of course, out of the question to use the box as a bed for the gull. However, there was no law against looking at it. She climbed on a chair and got it down.

She took the blue hat out carefully and laid it on the bed. All that tissue paper would certainly make a lovely soft nest. Maybe it wouldn't hurt to borrow the box for a little while. Of course she should go downstairs and ask permission first, but she had a strong conviction that the answer would be a firm " No." Still — if her mother didn't have the box, she'd manage with a bag or something. She always did.

The gull wouldn't need *all* that tissue paper. Taffy selected the largest piece and tucked it carefully around the blue hat and lifted hat and tissue to the closet shelf. Of course she would tell her mother what she had done, but that would have to wait until later. She rumpled the remaining tissue over the bottom of the box, making a lovely nest. Donna, she was sure, could have done no better. She carried the box down the hall and placed it beside Henry.

" Maybe this will do," she said eagerly.

Donna regarded the contribution. " I'll bet it's your mother's best hatbox."

Taffy did not explain that it was her mother's *only* hatbox at the moment. " Will it do? "

Henry's eyes seemed to hold something like approval. Taffy knew at once that no matter what trouble she got into over the box, the result was worth it. She wanted

Henry for a friend. She had a wishful vision of the four of them — David and Henry, Donna and Taffy — roaming the island together.

Then Celeste appeared on the stairs and this new sense of friendliness was gone.

"It is good that the gull will live," Celeste said. "But this is only the first warning."

Henry, carrying hatbox and gull, turned away from Taffy without a word. Donna picked up the candles and followed him downstairs. Taffy was left facing Celeste alone.

"It would be better if you and your mother would go away," the cook said. "Even the gulls do not want you here."

CHAPTER
⚹ 10 ⚸

Second Alarm

LATER in the afternoon the storm roared away with a final rush of wind and the sun came out in all the brilliance of a clear blue sky. But the island of Mackinac was strewed with the wreckage left behind.

Taffy wandered into the garden to find that most of the flower beds had been stripped of their blossoms. A big tree had gone down, and everywhere lay broken branches, wet leaves, and a scattering of twigs. Up the hillside were more broken trees, but the houses looked the same, and she could see the pointed roof of David's house poking up through the trees. At least that hadn't blown away.

She turned her attention to a stripped flower bed. It hurt to think how beautiful the garden had been yesterday. She knelt on the wet grass and tried to raise one of the plants to its original position. As she worked over it, she heard voices and looked around the bush that sheltered her to see Donna and Henry on the veranda with the hatbox between them. Probably they were getting ready to let the gull go.

She started over toward them; and then a memory of Henry's turning from her after Celeste had called the gull a warning and of Donna's following him downstairs held her back. They might not welcome her presence. She couldn't be sure.

As she waited uncertainly, Henry took the bird out of the box and set it on the veranda rail. The gull clung, its

wings fluttering. It seemed to have lost confidence, for it
made no effort to fly away. After a flutter or two, it sat
quite tamely on the rail. Tamely or timidly — Taffy wasn't
sure which.

"It got a bad bump and it doesn't trust the world any
more," Henry said.

Donna reached out a hand to the bird.

"Don't do that!" Henry pulled her back. The unexpected tug threw her off balance and she sat down hard
on the veranda floor.

No — not on the floor! Taffy heard the crackle of cardboard and tissue under Donna's weight and shivered at
the sound.

Donna was laughing as Henry pulled her to her feet, but
her laughter stopped abruptly. "Oh, dear!" she said. "I
hope Mrs. Saunders doesn't need that hatbox."

Taffy wanted to step out from behind the bush and as-
sure Donna that it was all right — even if that wasn't quite
true — but she knew she had waited too long. If she
popped out now, they might think she had been spying.

Donna picked up what was left of the hatbox, and she
and Henry went around toward the kitchen door.

When the sound of their voices died away, Taffy hurried out of hiding. The crushed box had been stuffed into
a trash basket outside the kitchen door; she pulled it out
with her heart sinking. One side had been bashed in and
torn halfway down. Well, she'd just have to carry it upstairs and see what Scotch tape and glue would do to put
it back in shape.

In her concern over the box she had forgotten the sea
gull. Now, as she came back around the corner of the
house, it gathered courage and spread its wings. Then in
mid-flight it faltered and dropped to the ground, mewing
pitifully — a very faint, "Help! Help!" Remembering
Henry's gentleness, Taffy crooned to it softly, talking to it

like the hurt baby thing it was. When she finally picked it up, it did not struggle. Its feathers were silky soft in her hands as she set it back in its tissue-paper nest. Even if the box no longer looked like a fitting place to keep a hat, it would still do as a nest for a sea gull.

Now — what next? Should she call Henry? But Mrs. Tuckerman had not wanted the gull around. She might order Donna to put it outside and it might die.

Up on the hillside the pointed tower of David's house seemed to beckon her. She scrambled to her feet, picked up the box, and started off. Now that she knew the way, the going seemed easier. The bird fluttered in the box, and she tried to hold it as carefully as she could.

In the goblin wood some of the dying trees had blown over, blocking her path. Underfoot the pine-needle carpet was like a wet sponge, and the bare tree boles had a black, wet sheen. The wood no longer frightened her. In her eagerness to reach David's she had no time to think of goblin shapes, or to worry about what might be hiding behind the next tree trunk. She hurried through the short cut, climbing over fallen tree trunks and going around those that were too big. The sun began to warm the earth, drinking up the moisture, and the pine had a wonderful smell.

To her surprise, David met her at the gate beneath the ship's lantern.

"I was looking through the glasses," he said, "and saw you start up the hill. What's in the box?"

She set it down on the walk and took off the cover. The gull fluttered frantically and then became quiet. Taffy told about the broken window, and the bird under the bed, and Celeste and Henry, and about the gull's apparent inability to fly.

"I thought maybe you could keep it here," Taffy said. "Do you think your grandmother would let you?"

"Sure," David said confidently. "I can keep it in the tower room. Gulls eat just about anything, I guess."

Taffy stroked the silver feathers gently and wondered why Henry had pulled Donna's hand away. "Henry said nothing was broken, but maybe its wing is sort of sprained and it needs to rest and grow strong again before it flies away."

"Your Aunt Martha would have known what to do," Mrs. Marsh said to Taffy when they showed her the gull. "After a storm they used to bring birds to her from all over the island. If they weren't hurt too badly, she knew how to make them well. I've heard her say she liked birds better than she liked most people."

"Oh," Taffy said, "did you know her?"

"Not well. Sometimes we went down to Sunset House to eat one of Celeste's good meals."

"I already asked grandma about the locked room," David said, "but she doesn't know anything about it."

"Did you know a man named Jeremiah Bogardus, Mrs. Marsh?" Taffy asked.

Mrs. Marsh thought a minute. "I met him at teas here and there. He was a good friend of Miss Irwin and the housekeeper at Sunset House. What's her name — Mrs. Tuckerman?"

Taffy was surprised. "A friend of Mrs. Tuckerman! But she wouldn't let him have a room at Sunset House."

"I had the impression that they used to like him," Mrs. Marsh said. "He was quite a traveler, I believe."

Taffy nodded. "He told us he lived all over the Orient." She stroked the bird, hating to leave it. This was almost like having a pet. "Do you think we could tame it, David? It doesn't seem to mind when I stroke it now. Maybe if it got to like us it wouldn't fly away at all."

"It'll be here for a while anyway," David said. "Let's be thinking about giving it a name."

Taffy left reluctantly and went down the hill. There was nothing for it but to abandon the hatbox. It no longer looked like anything her mother would want to keep a hat in. She hoped she would be able to slip back to the hotel unnoticed, but her mother's voice called to her as she crossed the wrecked garden.

"Taffy! Oh, Taffee-ee!"

"Here I am, mother. I only went up to David's."

Her mother leaned on the veranda rail. "Taffy, have you seen anything of my hatbox? I went up to the room just now and there was my blue hat sitting on the shelf with the box gone."

Taffy gulped. "I — I had to use it. I only meant to borrow it — honestly, I did. But then it got kind of — well — bent, and — "

"Use it! What ever for?"

"For a nest," Taffy said in a small voice. "A nest for the sea gull."

Mrs. Saunders waited for her daughter to come up on the veranda. "Perhaps I'm not very bright, but may I ask why you had to take my one and only hatbox when the storeroom of Sunset House is filled with any number of things that could very well be made into a bird's nest with no loss to anybody?"

How, Taffy wondered, could she make her mother see that this had been a very urgent matter? If they'd got something from the storeroom, then Donna would have provided the nest, and she'd have lost a chance to win Henry's regard.

"Well?" Mrs. Saunders said, waiting.

"I'm sorry." Taffy sighed. "I — I guess it just seemed like a good idea at the time."

"I know where there's a hatbox." Henry Fox's voice came from high in the garden.

Taffy saw him looking down at them from the branches

of a tree that grew close to the building. He held a saw in one hand and apparently had been cutting off branches broken by the storm. He propped the saw in a crotch and came nimbly down the tree.

"Miss Irwin had some old hatboxes," he told them. " I can get one for you."

" Thank you, Henry," Mrs. Saunders said. " That will be fine." She turned back to her daughter. " Do you suppose that next time you get one of these wonderful, terribly urgent inspirations you could first take two minutes and ask me about it? " But she was smiling and Taffy knew she had been forgiven again.

She flew after Henry to learn where the hatboxes were kept, making worthy promises to herself. Oh, she *would* ask next time! Mother had every right to be annoyed. Goodness! If *she* ever had a daughter whose crazy ideas always led to trouble, it would certainly serve her right. From now on she was going to do better. Oh, very much better!

She had to hurry to keep up with Henry as he ran up two flights of stairs to the third floor. A small door she had not tried before was near the head of the stairs, and Henry opened it without hesitation. Apparently none of the house's secrets were hidden from him. Probably he even knew what was in the locked room.

The small door led to another flight of stairs, steep and narrow, going up into the dim reaches of the house. A musty, mysterious, shut-in smell greeted her as she climbed upward behind Henry. At the top he fumbled a moment and found the pull chain of an overhead bulb. The electric damage caused by the storm had been repaired and the light revealed a long attic poked up under the main roof. Old trunks and boxes were arranged in neat, orderly fashion. In the middle of the floor was a stationary ladder leading to a trap door in the roof. Probably that went up

to the railed platform she had seen from David's house —
the one he'd called a "widow's walk."

As she stood looking around, Henry seemed to notice
her for the first time. He gave her a long, slow look that
was neither friendly nor unfriendly.

"Hi," he said — just that one word — and walked over
to a stack of boxes. After a moment's rummaging, he held
out a small, sturdy hatbox. "Do you think this one'll do?"

"Oh, yes!" Taffy breathed. She would have said yes to
anything he held up — from a lamp shade to an egg box.
Fortunately for her recent resolutions, it was a good box.

"I'm sorry you got into trouble over the other one,"
Henry said gravely. He walked back toward the hanging
bulb.

"Wait a minute!" Taffy cried. She had not meant to
question the Indian boy, but now that the words were out
she knew she had to go on. She fumbled with the cord of

the hatbox, as if action of some sort would help her. When words did come, she blurted them out breathlessly.

"Why don't you want us here, Henry? Why did you stick that note on the tree up in the wood? Why do you look at me sometimes as if you didn't like me?"

Henry seemed uncomfortable, even a little unhappy. "I guess you're all right," he said. "I like the way you helped with the gull."

"Then why, Henry — *why* — ?"

His hand moved toward the bulb. "Mrs. Tuckerman and Celeste and Donna have been good to me," he said. "I want things to turn out right for them." His fingers found the chain and the attic went dark.

There was nothing for Taffy to do but take the hatbox and go downstairs. Asking questions had got her nowhere. How *could* anything turn out wrong for Celeste and Mrs. Tuckerman and Donna if mother did a good job with the hotel? Why did so many people want her to fail?

At dinner Mrs. Tuckerman talked about the damage the storm had done to Mackinac. When Donna said she was sorry she had broken the hatbox, Taffy was glad to tell her about the box Henry had found but did not let her know she had seen the accident.

After dinner Taffy looked at all the picture magazines in the lounge that she had not looked at before, and then picked up an old book about the island. As she turned the page a familiar word caught her eye — the word "Cannon." This time it had nothing to do with cannons at the fort, or, in fact, with any real cannon. It was a story about a restaurant, the Cannon Ball, that had been very popular in the '90's. The cook had been a French-Canadian woman named Celeste Cloutier who could produce what the book called "culinary miracles." This Celeste Cloutier, Taffy knew, was the mother of the Sunset House Celeste.

Perhaps when Celeste spoke about the "Cannon," she

was shortening the name " Cannon Ball." Perhaps that was where the key had been hidden. Now that this new idea had seized her, she could hardly wait until tomorrow to talk it over with David.

The hotel remained quiet until a quarter to nine. Mrs. Saunders had just said, " Taffy, bedtime," when Henry Fox came downstairs and over to her chair.

" Miss Twig wants you," he said in an undertone.

Mrs. Saunders gave him a quick look.

" I think she's upset," Henry added.

Taffy, curious, followed her mother upstairs. Miss Clara was seated limply in a chair, wrapped in a flannel dressing gown, her hair done up in paper curlers and her face pale. Miss Hattie leaned over one of the room's two beds.

" Isn't it queer? " she said. " All those little bones set together in a sort of pattern! How do you suppose they got into Clara's bed? "

Miss Clara was more dramatic. " A skeleton! " she cried. " A skeleton in my bed! This is the end. We are leaving at once. My sister has a weak heart and I cannot subject her to these shocks."

What looked to be the white bones of a tiny skeleton lay neatly on the clean, smooth sheet.

Miss Hattie's weak heart did not seem to be bothering her at the moment. " It's some small animal, isn't it? " she asked. " A flying animal, I'd say."

Mrs. Saunders nodded soberly. " I think it's the skeleton of a bat. But how it got *here* — ! "

Mrs. Tuckerman, who had joined them, closed the door against the possible curiosity of guests passing in the hall.

" This must be some child's prank," she said.

Taffy thought about her words. Could Donna have played a trick like this? Then she saw that her mother was watching her.

Mrs. Saunders took a sheet of hotel writing paper from

the desk and slid it carefully under the collection of bones. They slipped easily onto the paper.

"I'm sorry this happened," she told the Twigs. "I shall certainly try to get to the bottom of it." But she sounded discouraged.

"We'll dress and leave at once," Miss Clara said tartly.

"There's no need to leave at this hour. Perhaps if you could move to another room for tonight —" She looked questioningly at Mrs. Tuckerman, but the housekeeper shook her head.

"We haven't a vacant room in the place."

"Then you may have my room," Mrs. Saunders offered. "For tonight Taffy and I can sleep downstairs on cots."

Miss Hattie looked hopefully at her sister. "That would be very kind of Mrs. Saunders. Perhaps you'll feel better tomorrow, Clara, and we won't need to leave."

"I shall *not* feel better," her sister announced. "But if it will make you happier, I shall accept Mrs. Saunders' offer to move us to her room for the night."

"I'll get the room ready," Mrs. Saunders said, and went off carrying the paper with the tiny skeleton on it. Taffy, walking at her mother's side, looked curiously at the bones.

Mrs. Tuckerman followed them into the hall. "There's no need to make yourself uncomfortable. My room has two beds; you might as well use one of them. Donna and Taffy can sleep on the cots downstairs."

Taffy forgot the skeleton for a moment and gave a pleased squeal. "Oh, mother! Do let's fix it that way. It will be sort of like camping out. Please, let's!"

"I'm sure Donna would like it," Mrs. Tuckerman said.

But before the two girls moved downstairs, Taffy and her mother had a moment alone. Taffy was helping to put fresh sheets on the beds the Twigs were to occupy.

"Taffy," Mrs. Saunders said quietly, "you didn't put that bat skeleton in Miss Twig's bed, did you?"

Taffy paused, a pillow against her chest, and looked at her mother in astonishment. "Of course not! Why ever would you think I'd do such an awful thing?"

Her mother sighed in relief. "I didn't really think you would. I've never known you to have an unkind sense of humor. In fact, I don't agree with Mrs. Tuckerman that this is the sort of thing a child would do. I don't know what to think. I don't know what to think at all."

If it wasn't a child's prank, Taffy decided, it couldn't have been Donna. But somebody had put the skeleton there. Who?

CHAPTER
⊁ 11 ⊰

Awakening in the Dark

COTS were set up in Aunt Martha's office next to the locked room. When Donna and Taffy had been tucked under the blankets with the usual motherly directions to go to sleep right away (as if that were possible!), and Mrs. Tuckerman and Mrs. Saunders had gone upstairs, Donna sat up and swung her pajama-clad legs over the side of her cot.

The office door had been left ajar, and a bar of light from the lounge slanted across one corner so that the room was not entirely dark. It was after ten o'clock, and most of the Sunset House guests had gone to bed. Mrs. Harrison, one of the younger guests, was reading in the lounge, while her husband played checkers with Colonel Linwood. The light in the lounge would burn all night, for which Taffy was secretly thankful.

" I'm hungry," Donna said, " and I'm not a bit sleepy. We should have asked for something to eat. I suppose we could go out to the kitchen and see what we could find."

Taffy was doubtful. " The Harrisons and Colonel Linwood would see us."

" Suppose they did? "

" Well — it's just that we're sort of under suspicion."

Donna looked startled. " Suspicion? What for? "

" *Somebody* put that bat skeleton in Miss Twig's bed.

Your mother said it was a child's prank, and we're the only children here. Maybe we'd better not go running around when we're supposed to be in bed."

Donna was silent for a moment, and Taffy wished the light from the lounge were brighter so that she could see the other girl's face more clearly. Then Donna put her bare feet on the floor and went over and turned on the green desk lamp. Mrs. Saunders had brought the tiny set of bones downstairs and left them on Aunt Martha's desk. Donna bent over the paper and poked the bones around, and Taffy knelt on her cot the better to see.

"You know something?" Donna said. And as Taffy waited breathlessly: "Somebody's fixed this up. It's wired together with fine little wires so that it won't fall apart."

Taffy joined Donna at the desk. Even though she had been told the wires were there, she had to look closely to see them.

"It's like something fixed up for a museum," she said. "Whoever would do a thing like that?"

Donna nodded in the direction of the "J.B." picture of Aunt Martha and the birds that had been replaced on the wall. "She would. She liked to fix things like this."

"Then it was in the hotel," Taffy said, "and must have been taken by someone who knew about it."

Donna lowered her voice. "Maybe *she* took it — Miss Irwin, I mean. Maybe *she* put it in Miss Twig's bed."

Taffy shivered and the next moment laughed at her own uneasiness. "I'm not Miss Twig, and I'm not Celeste. I don't believe in things like that."

"I guess I don't either," Donna confessed. "But it's too late to stop the Twigs from leaving. Celeste says this is just the beginning. Maybe everybody will leave."

This time Taffy's uneasiness was real. "Then what will happen?"

Donna returned to her cot and sat cross-legged on the

covers. "Mother thinks the place will go to the birds."

"You said that once before. What birds?"

"Oh, probably some bird society that will turn it into a haven, or a museum, or a home for sick birds, or something."

Taffy didn't think much of the idea. Birds were all right and she liked them. In fact, she loved the baby sea gull. But she couldn't help feeling that birds would get along all right outdoors, while the Saunderses needed a home.

"Of course," Donna went on, "Celeste doesn't think Miss Irwin really went that far. She doesn't think the birds will get it at all."

"*Who* does she think will get it?" Taffy demanded.

"My mother," Donna said calmly. "Miss Irwin meant it to go to her in the first place. She had the will drawn up and everything, and then they had a quarrel and she changed the will."

Taffy got back into bed and pulled the covers over her. She had a lot to think about.

"Anyway, it's all guesswork," Donna said. "Miss Irwin was smart as anything, but sort of queer, and she just loved to run everybody. She always thought she knew exactly what people ought to do. She got awfully mad when they wouldn't do what she said."

"I know." Taffy nodded. "She didn't want my mother to marry my father and wouldn't have anything more to do with her when she did. That's why it was such a surprise about the will."

After that Taffy was silent, thinking her own thoughts, and Donna went to sleep. Taffy listened to her regular breathing and thought about the mystery of the locked room so near at hand, and about the day the final portion of Aunt Martha's will would be read. If the Saunderses didn't make good at running it, would Sunset House go to the birds, as Mrs. Tuckerman seemed to think it might, or to the Tuckermans, as Celeste believed? Or would Aunt Martha have played a queer joke and done something completely unexpected with it?

She thought too about the tiny wired bat skeleton and whether Donna might, after all, have put it in Miss Twig's bed. Could Henry Fox be mixed up in this? And what of the Cannon Ball? She meant to ask David about that to-morrow.

Out in the lounge the checker game came to an end. The Harrisons and Colonel Linwood went upstairs, and silence settled over Sunset House. Again Taffy was glad a light burned in the lounge. In a way the light was company. Then her eyelids grew heavy and she slipped into dreams.

She came awake suddenly, feeling as if some sound had exploded practically in her ears. For a moment she could not remember where she was. The windows, faintly lighted patches, were not where the windows should be, and everything seemed jumbled about and in the wrong places. Then she remembered that she was not in her room upstairs, but in Aunt Martha's office, and almost at once came the realization that the lounge was dark. Had the electricity failed again? Or had someone turned out the light? It was supposed to burn all night. Mother had said it always did.

She sat up in bed, her heart beginning to thump. Something was strange; something was wrong. Stretching, she reached across for Donna. There was no one in the other bed — only rumpled sheets and a pillow dented by a head that no longer rested against it.

Taffy got out of bed, suddenly panicky. As she fumbled her way across the room, she bumped into unexpected furniture and became hopelessly confused. Nothing, apparently, was where it belonged. The door to the lounge should have been ajar, but when her trembling fingers touched the panel she knew the door was closed. She felt for the knob, found it, turned it, and the door opened.

A sharp, stuffy smell engulfed her, and she had a frightened realization of what she had done. In her confusion she had turned the wrong way and reached the door of the locked room; only now it was not locked, but had opened at once to her touch. Abruptly she recognized the sound that had awakened her. It had been a key turning harshly in a stiff lock. She was on the threshold of the mysterious room.

There in the stillness and darkness the knowledge was too frightening to face.

She drew the door quickly shut to close in whatever might be there and flung herself toward the lounge. The room had turned into an unknown hazard. She bumped her shins against a cot and stumbled over a chair before she reached the other door. Every trace of memory about how the furniture was placed had vanished from her mind. Somehow she bumped her way to the stairs, and had reached the third step on her upward flight when the light in the lounge came on.

" What ever are you doing? " Donna's voice demanded in a whisper.

Weakly Taffy clung to the rail. Donna stood in the hallway below, her dark, curly hair ruffled and her hands filled with sandwiches which she had not bothered to put on a plate.

" Are you trying to wake everybody up? " Donna went on, still in a whisper. " The whole house will be down in a minute, and then they'll tell us we shouldn't be eating in the middle of the night."

Taffy came down the stairs, her teeth chattering. " D-d-did you turn off the light? " she asked.

"Of course. I didn't want anybody to catch me running around down here."

"Did *you* unlock that door?" Taffy went on, her knees weak as she walked toward Donna.

"What door?" Donna asked, and Taffy could not be sure whether the blank look she wore was real, or had been put there to hide whatever she might know.

Taffy did not repeat her question. With lights on again, and Donna standing there with very real sandwiches in her hands, she was no longer frightened. She walked into the office and straight to the mysterious door. But now the door was locked securely.

"Is that the door you mean?" Donna asked. "You've been dreaming. That door's always been locked."

Taffy stared at its blank surface. *Had* she been dreaming? Had she only thought she had opened it?

But, no. The sharp, queer odor lingered in the office. Now that she was no longer terrified she recognized the odor of moth balls. That was funny. What was in the room that Aunt Martha had wanted to preserve from moths?

It was the odor that made her sure her experience had been no dream. She *had* opened the door. A few moments ago it had not been locked and someone had been in the locked-away room. Was it Donna? Donna might have come from the kitchen, and she might not. She might have gone to the kitchen earlier and had the sandwiches with her when she went into the room.

Donna seemed to be watching her sharply. "You look as though you'd had an awful scare. Here — have a sandwich. I made enough for both of us."

Taffy took a peanut-butter sandwich, but though Donna munched hungrily, she could not eat at all. A single mouthful almost choked her; her fright was too recent, too vivid, and her stomach still too shaky for food.

"You know," Donna said, "I've been thinking about

what you told me. I mean about Miss Irwin not wanting your mother to marry your father. Something like that happened with my mother too."

Taffy waited. This time she hoped Donna would go on talking. The quivering in her stomach began to quiet.

"A few years ago my mother knew a man she liked pretty well," Donna went on. "I liked him too. He was swell. But Miss Irwin interfered and got her to send him away. Here — do you like bologna?"

Taffy shook her head. "Aunt Martha sounds like an awfully unpleasant person."

Donna thought about that. "No, she wasn't unpleasant, but you never knew what she'd do next. She could be awfully good to people. She set aside a trust fund for Henry, so he'll have money for his medical training when he gets out of high school."

"Did she do that?" Taffy was amazed.

Donna nodded. "Henry's father died when he was small and his mother died a few years ago. Celeste knew his mother and she took care of him. It was Celeste who got him a job here and got Miss Irwin interested in him."

"But if Aunt Martha liked being good to people, why didn't she want you to be a dancer?"

"She just didn't approve of it, I guess. That's what she and mother quarreled about." Donna put a last wedge of sandwich into her mouth and clasped her hands about her drawn-up knees. "There isn't anything in the whole world I want more than to be a dancer. I don't care how hard it will be. A dancer has to practice and work awfully hard if she wants to be really good."

"You *are* good," Taffy assured her.

"No, I'm not; not really. I'm only beginning. But I'm going to be good someday. Dancing lessons cost a lot of money. That's why it would be so wonderful if what Celeste says is true, that the will might leave the hotel to us."

Taffy felt a little sad. Donna Tuckerman wanted to be a dancer as much as she wanted a home and a room of her own. But one of them had to lose. They couldn't both win.

" Celeste thinks Miss Irwin shouldn't have acted the way she did," Donna went on. "After all, you're outsiders. Your mother hasn't been here since she was a little girl. Celeste says the gulls know. She says the house knows and will make you leave."

Taffy didn't want to hear any more. She lay down with her back to Donna and pulled up the covers. Donna didn't sound mean or angry, but Taffy didn't want to hear the things she was saying. Everything would be so much nicer, she thought, if they could all be happy together and get what each one wanted.

She lay awake in the darkness, watching the ribbon of light from the lounge. She had learned a lot tonight and she had had a scare. But what to make of it all she didn't know in the least.

CHAPTER

❧ 12 ❧

At British Landing

TAFFY awoke to find her mother standing beside the cot.

"Up with you, sleepyhead. Donna had breakfast an hour ago."

As she dressed, Taffy sniffed the air several times. The smell of moth balls had disappeared from the office, and in the bright light of morning sunshine last night seemed distant and unreal. *Had* she got out of bed, and fumbled her way to the door and actually opened it?

She crossed the room and tried it once more without success. As she stared at its blank surface she saw a bit of gray caught in the door about halfway up. She picked at it until it came loose and carried it to the light to examine it carefully. It was a silver-gray feather. It might have belonged to the gull she and David had adopted, except that it could not have come from that gull. But it was the feather of a sea gull — that was certain.

And it meant just one thing. The door *had* been open last night; the rasping of the key in the lock *had* awakened her. Whoever had opened the door *had* been in the room. Probably, alarmed by the noise she had made bumping her way to the stairs, the unknown had relocked the door and had caught the feather of a sea gull between door and frame.

But who? Donna? Donna was the only other person she

knew had been downstairs at that late hour. Or had it
been someone who had locked the door from the inside,
had hidden in the room, and had escaped later when she
and Donna were asleep? If it hadn't been Donna, who
could it have been?

The moment demanded immediate action, and to that
there was only one answer. Before going in to a late breakfast, she ran upstairs and hung her mother's best green
sweater in the window. She and David had decided on
still another signal. Green meant, " Come as soon as you
can."

She finished a lonely breakfast and came out of the
dining room in time to see the Twigs leaving, bag and
baggage. She watched a determined Miss Clara get firmly
into Sam's carriage, but it seemed to Taffy that Miss Harriet looked back at Sunset House regretfully.

Taffy was still on the veranda when David, responding
to the green signal, turned his bicycle up the hotel driveway.

" What's up? " he asked the moment he saw her.

Taffy waved limply in the direction of the departing
Twigs.

" Somebody put a bat in Miss Clara's bed last night, and
after the storm, and the gull and everything, she decided
it was too much."

" Look," David said patiently, " maybe you'd better begin at the beginning."

" I will," Taffy promised. " But first tell me something.
Have you ever heard of a place called the Cannon Ball? "

" Sure. In the old days it used to be a restaurant, but
now it's just an old, deserted building up at British Landing."

Taffy explained her interest in the Cannon Ball, leaving
the rest of the story for later.

" If you had a bike," David said, " we could ride there

this morning. Why don't you see if your mother will let you rent one?"

Mrs. Saunders agreed and telephoned the place that rented them. Taffy and David started for the village at once, David pushing his bicycle along the road and Taffy walking beside him.

On the way she told him everything that had happened, starting with the discovery of the little bat skeleton in Miss Twig's bed. David made no comment until she told him about opening the door in the dark. She tried to make him understand how frightening the discovery had been, so that he would see why she hadn't gone into the room. But he was scornful and unbelieving.

"You mean you had the door open," he cried, "and you didn't do anything about finding out what was inside? You just closed it and ran away?"

Taffy could only nod.

David whistled. "You'll never get a chance like that again. That's the trouble with girls — they get scared at the wrong time."

"Maybe you'd have been scared too," Taffy told him indignantly. "If you're going to talk about the 'trouble with girls,' I won't tell you one word more. And there *is* more."

"O. K.," he said, grinning at her. "But I just wish I'd been there and had your chance."

She took the feather from the pocket of her dress and held it out to him. "If you're so smart, see what you can make of this for a clue."

"It looks like one from Grayfeather," David said.

"Grayfeather?"

"The gull. You know — we were going to think up a name. Have you got a better one?"

"I haven't had time to think about one," Taffy admitted.

"Grayfeather sounds fine to me. But this couldn't be one

of his. I found it stuck in the locked door."

They reached the bicycle place and Taffy made a careful choice of the wheel she would ride all summer. The one she selected was bright blue, with balloon tires and a wire basket over the handle bars.

"Let's go by way of the top of the island," David said when they were ready to start. "We'll get a long downhill run that way and can come home by the shore road along the water."

Getting to the heights meant a steep climb up the wide road that led past the Grand Hotel. Behind the famous hotel's big white columns a long veranda stretched across the entire front of the building, and at the end of the veranda nearest the road a woman sat in a rocking chair. Taffy recognized Miss Hattie Twig and wondered if solving the multiplying mysteries might bring the Twigs back to Sunset House.

David got the whole story as they pushed their bikes up the steep incline.

"In mystery stories you always count over the suspects and see what motives they have," he said wisely. "Then the one you never expected at all turns out to be guilty. And the one you suspected from the first turns out to be innocent."

"I don't know who to suspect or not to suspect," Taffy said. "I suppose Donna *could* have been in that room last night. There wasn't anybody else around, as far as I know. If she had a key, she could have unlocked the door and locked it again."

"She couldn't have if you hadn't run away," David pointed out.

This time Taffy didn't argue. "But I can't see why it would be Donna, anyway. And who could have put the bat bones in the bed?"

"Who else could be a suspect? I don't mean somebody

you saw downstairs last night. I mean anybody around the hotel."

"Well — there's Henry Fox. Celeste has been good to him, so he'd be loyal to her. Celeste has said right out that she doesn't want us there. Besides, you know Indians. They can sneak around and never even make a twig crackle."

"You're thinking of book Indians — real Indians are like anybody else. And there aren't any twigs to crackle on the floor at Sunset House."

"There's Celeste," Taffy went on, ignoring this. "Maybe she makes the best suspect, since she thinks we're not good for Sunset House."

"What about Mrs. Tuckerman?" David asked.

Taffy paused for breath. "Whew! Won't we ever get to the top? No, I don't think Mrs. Tuckerman has anything to do with it. Maybe she'd like to see mother fail, but I don't think she'd really try to do anything about it."

"There you are!" David announced. "It must be Tuckerman. It's always the one you don't suspect."

Taffy shook her head. "Now *you're* talking like a book. Besides, there's still one more person we can least suspect. Mr. Bogardus."

"Oh, him!" David dismissed Mr. Bogardus. "He's O. K. Besides, he isn't staying at the hotel. Well, here we are at the top." David dismissed the suspects for the moment and turned to the immediate pleasure of the ride ahead. "I brought a map along if you want to look at the road."

Taffy put down the kick stand on her bike and went over to look at the somewhat limp and rumpled paper he spread against the handle bars.

"Here's British Landing," he said, "nearly at the farthest point of the island, and there's British Landing Road. We can take Indian Road, or Wigwam Trail, or Custer Road to run into it."

The way they took wound through thick woods, more
a lane than a road. Leaves and pine needles strewed the
way, making a springy bed along which the bicycles rolled
with surprising smoothness.

This was wonderful, Taffy thought, lifting her face to
the sun and the brisk cool breeze. The lane wound and
dipped before it straightened into the long downhill
stretch of British Landing Road. They coasted down the
long incline from the heights — the " turtle's back " of the
island — clear to the water's edge.

The last hill was a steep drop and Taffy used her brake.
Ahead of her, David had dismounted and set his bicycle
safely off the road where it would not be in the way of
carriages. The stony beach formed a shallow bay, and
there was a picnic table and rustic benches, but Taffy
chose to sit on a fallen log.

" Why do they call it British Landing? " she wanted to
know.

" Because that's what the British did," David explained.
" They landed here in the night and crossed the island to
take the fort. But the Americans didn't fight. They laid
down their arms and let the British in."

" Why? " asked Taffy.

" It was smarter not to. The Indian tribes had promised
to help the British if the Americans offered any resistance.
The Americans weren't strong enough and there'd have
been a massacre. Later the Americans tried the same trick.
They landed here and there was a battle up on the meadow
at the top of the hill. The Americans were driven back and
lost a lot of men. You can see the graves in the old ceme-
tery. But we won the war and the fort came to America
anyway."

Taffy rocked back and forth on the log with her eyes
half closed. She could almost see the boats coming in to
the beach and the soldiers jumping out of them. Strange

to sit here in this peaceful, quiet spot, with the waves lapping gently against the pebbles, and imagine the stormy scenes that had been enacted here in days long past.

"We're closer to the mainland here than anywhere else on the island," David said. "That's St. Ignace across the water."

Taffy pulled herself out of the past. "Where is the Cannon Ball?" That was mainly what they had come to see.

David pointed. "Right there across the road."

Taffy wasn't sure what she had expected. The name "Cannon Ball" had a romantic sound, but the reality was disappointing. The low building looked neglected to the point of sad ruin.

"Poor old thing," Taffy said softly. "I wonder if it gets lonesome for the old days? Let's pay it a visit and cheer it up."

David gave her a look, but said nothing, as though he had grown used to her imaginings. They crossed the road and circled the dilapidated old place. The veranda was screened, but a large section of the screening had rusted away and left a hole big enough to walk through.

"Come on," David said.

Taffy climbed after him through the hole. The veranda was wide, and in Taffy's imagination there were ghostly tables all about her, with ladies seated at them, in old-fashioned clothes, chatting to their mustached escorts. She could smell the scent of their perfume, and wonderful odors of cooking — the cooking of that other Celeste who had brought people here to taste her fine dishes.

"Look," David said, "if you'd just stick around and not go skittering back about fifty or a hundred years all the time, I could keep track of you better. We're here to find out about a key — remember?"

The tables vanished and the scent of perfume was gone.

Underfoot the veranda was strewed with rotting bark and rusty-brown pine needles. In places the roof looked ready to fall. David and Taffy moved cautiously around the corner of the house.

Some of the windows that opened upon the veranda were blocked by blinds. Others had faded, yellow newspapers pasted over them. A pane in one window was broken, and they looked in on a big empty room. A curtained door was hung with faded chintz on which flowers had once marked a gay pattern. From a hook on the wall hung a woman's mildewed apron, forgotten, perhaps, by the last cook to leave the Cannon Ball.

But David's concern was with the present, not the past. "If this was the 'Cannon' Celeste meant, how would it hide the secret of the key? What do you think she meant?"

Taffy had no idea. "All we can do is look around for a hiding place. Besides, the key may not be there. A key was used to open the door last night."

Before they could begin their search, they heard the sound of hoofs and carriage wheels. Instead of going by, the carriage turned up British Landing Road and stopped. The Cannon Ball was drawing more than one visitor today.

"Sh-sh!" Taffy warned. "Who is it?"

They tiptoed to the corner of the veranda and peered around it cautiously. Taffy put a quick hand to her mouth. A figure in dungarees and beaded moccasins was getting out of the carriage.

"It's Celeste," she whispered. "She's got the hotel carriage, but she's alone!"

Paying no attention to the house, Celeste hurried across the weed-thick yard toward the rear. By walking softly along the veranda Taffy and David were able to keep her in sight.

They saw her drop to her knees beside a tree and

reach into what must have been a hollow. Her hand, when she withdrew it, held a small box. She carried the box toward the road.

Taffy, more excited than David, and stepping less carefully, put her foot down on a rotting board that broke with a sharp crack. The sound stopped Celeste short and she sent a startled look toward the house. Taffy, knowing that concealment was no longer possible, stepped through the broken screen.

"Hi, Celeste! It's only us."

Celeste frowned as they joined her in the yard.

"Well!" she exclaimed. "And what are you doing here, you two?"

Taffy tried to smile. Probably it was better to tell the truth than to hide their purpose.

"This is my friend David Marsh," she said. "We came here to look for the key."

"Key?" Celeste held the little box tighter.

"You said the Cannon hid the secret of the key. So we figured it had to be either at the fort or the Cannon Ball."

"Very smart," Celeste said through thinning lips. "Very smart indeed. And what would you do if you had the key?"

"We'd open the locked room," Taffy said boldly.

Celeste shook the little box and something metallic rattled inside. "A good thing I got to it first! Because do you know what I am going to do?"

She turned toward the beach and they hurried after her. At the water's edge Celeste stopped.

"Since you are here," she said, "you can watch. I am going to fling the key far out into the lake where it will never be found again."

"But why?" David said. "Why?"

Water lapped the toes of Celeste's moccasins as she held the box dramatically toward the sky. "There are things it

is better not to release until their power is weak and old. If there is no key, Mrs. Saunders will not trouble about the room until the end of the season. To her it means only unimportant work that can be delayed. She does not understand these old, evil things as I do."

She opened the little box and took out a key. Brass flashed in the sunlight as she raised her hand.

"But there's another key," Taffy cried. "So what good will it do to throw this one away?"

Celeste paused, her hand still raised. "There is only one key. I hold it here in my hand."

"There must be another key because somebody had the door open last night."

"What?" Celeste demanded, bringing her hand down from its dramatic pose. "What are you talking about?"

"Somebody opened the door when I was downstairs last night," Taffy said, "and then locked it again."

Slowly Celeste opened her hand and looked long and closely at the key. Her eyes were all at once dark and frightened.

"There has been a substitution. Someone has tried to fool me. This is not the right key. Did you do this? Did you change the keys? Do you have the other one?"

"Of course not," Taffy said indignantly. "We only just got here. We hadn't even started to look."

Celeste gave her a brooding stare, slipped the little box into the pocket of her dungarees, and strode back to the carriage. Settled in the driver's seat, she turned the horses about and started along the shore road without a backward glance.

"She's crazy," David said. "She's completely nuts."

"No." Taffy shook her head. "She's different, that's all. She's lived so close to the island and its history and stories that she believes the things the Indians used to believe which don't seem sensible to us."

David's grunt neither agreed nor disagreed.

"Goodness!" Taffy went on, warming to her subject. "Sometimes people think things about me because I see what isn't really there. That's just imagination. Celeste has an extra-big supply of it."

But she could see that David wasn't going to be convinced. There was nothing to do now except start back to Sunset House.

It was while they were pedaling along the level shore road that David got the idea about the *voyageurs*.

CHAPTER
⚹ 13 ⚹

Wings Again

OF COURSE we wouldn't use boats," David said, explaining his idea to Taffy.

Taffy pedaled along beside him, not paying much attention because she was thinking out loud. " I guess this lets Celeste out as a suspect. If she thought the key was still hidden at the Cannon Ball, she couldn't have been the one who opened the door."

" But we could make trips," David went on, " just like the *voyageurs* used to do. Maybe we could be a sort of club and call ourselves *Voyageurs*."

" I wonder who could have changed those keys? " Taffy pondered. " I wonder who else Celeste could have told about the Cannon hiding a secret? " She came out of her preoccupation to catch an echo of David's last words. " Call ourselves what? What are you talking about? "

" The *Voyageurs*," David said, giving her a disgusted look. " We could have a club and take trips to historic places on the island like we did today to British Landing."

Taffy, her interest at last aroused, was full of the idea when they rolled up in front of Sunset House.

" Hello, you two," Mrs. Saunders called from the porch. " Nearly time for lunch."

" Could David stay, mother? " Taffy asked. " We're right in the middle of plans and we need to get them finished."

Mrs. Saunders smiled. " I wish you'd put that imagina-

tion of yours to work on plans to keep our guests happy
and take their minds off gulls and bats."

Taffy looked at David. "The *Voyageurs* Club!" she
cried. "Why couldn't guests belong to it? I mean grownups. We needn't use bikes. We could have a — a conducted
hiking tour, maybe, and take a lunch and have a picnic."

David caught the idea at once. "We could start 'em out
on an easy trip — to Arch Rock."

"You're going too fast for me," Mrs. Saunders said helplessly. "Perhaps you'd better save it for after lunch.
David, suppose you telephone your grandmother and ask
if you may stay." The sound of the dining-room doors being opened reached the porch. "Taffy, I promised I'd let
you ring the gong. Go ahead if you'd like to."

Taffy flew into the house and picked up the padded
stick that hung from the gong stand. She struck the gong
a blow and heard a crash of sound go echoing through the
house. She could feel her cheeks go warm with embarrass-
ment at the unexpected boom. She struck the gong again,
this time gently. She hadn't expected the little gong to
have such a powerful voice. Tapped gently, its summons
was musical.

David, seated at Taffy's table, soon made friends with
Donna. Lunch time was a livelier meal than usual, and
Taffy found herself wishing David could eat at the hotel
every day.

"We could put up an announcement of the first trip on
the bulletin board in the lounge," Donna suggested when
Taffy told her of the club.

"Maybe mother would let me type a notice on Miss
Irwin's machine in the office," Taffy said eagerly. "I used
to use daddy's typewriter sometimes, though I can only
do it with two fingers."

"When'll we have the first trip?" Donna asked. "Tomorrow?"

David shook his head. "Tomorrow's boat day, and the island will be jammed. It's no fun trying to go to any of the popular places on boat day."

Taffy nodded agreement. She was beginning to feel like the old-timers — a little superior toward tourists who rushed in for a day and then rushed breathlessly out again.

The trip to Arch Rock was set for the day after tomorrow — if they could sign up enough *Voyageurs*. After lunch the three of them went to the kitchen and asked Celeste if she would pack box lunches.

Celeste, busy preparing a sauce, did not look at them. "So it has come to this! Sandwiches and picnics. Ha!"

"You'll pack nice boxes, won't you?" Taffy pleaded.

"Sandwiches!" Celeste lifted the pan from the stove. "Picnics!" She threw back her dark head. "Something has got out of that room. I feel it. They loved Miss Irwin; they trusted her. They do not understand these new people. They do not like those who frighten them with gongs."

Taffy felt herself shrink. Not because she believed the gong could frighten whatever was in the room, but because of her bungling.

Practical David, who had accepted the gong's uproar as something that happened every day, asked a question, "Who doesn't like what?"

But Celeste was again absorbed with her sauce and did not answer.

"Let her alone," Donna whispered, and drew Taffy and David from the kitchen. "She didn't say she wouldn't fix the lunch. You know something? We ought to have a guide for the trip."

"I know the way," David told her. "And I bet you do too. Why do we need a guide?"

"I mean a real Indian guide. Why don't we ask Henry Fox?"

Taffy seized on the idea with enthusiasm. "Let's ask him now."

They found Henry working in the garden.

"I'll play guide, if you want me to," he agreed readily. "How'd you like me to wear feathers?"

It seemed to Taffy there was a barb in his voice.

"Stop laughing at us," Donna scolded. "You know more about the island than we do. That's why we asked you."

"Besides," Taffy put in quickly, "we want members for our *Voyageurs* Club and we'd like you to join."

Henry gave her a slow smile. Anyway, the barb was gone. This was working out as she had hoped, so that they'd all be friends doing things together.

Mrs. Tuckerman called Donna, and David went home. Taffy put a pencil and paper into her pocket and went out to a corner of the porch. Curled up in a chair, she considered the wording of the announcement she meant to post on the hotel bulletin board. After a number of false starts and the crossing out of many words, she had an announcement she thought might do.

THE VOYAGEURS CLUB

Invites you on a guided trip to Arch Rock. Sunset House will fix lunches for everybody.

Climb the Indian trails that lead to the Rock and hear an Indian guide tell you the legends about it.

Register with Taffy Saunders if you want to go.

Later, with her mother's permission to use the typewriter, she went into the office and tried the door once more. It was getting to be a habit to try that door. It was locked, just as she had expected. She wondered what investigating Celeste might have done about the substituted key.

Rummaging through the drawers of Aunt Martha's desk, she found typewriter paper for the notice. The job took several sheets, because at first it was hard to get the words centered on the page so that they looked neat, and her fingers kept hitting the wrong keys. But eventually the task was done to her satisfaction.

In one of her rummaging searches for paper and an eraser she had come upon a big square notebook and had left it out on the desk. Notebooks fascinated her. Daddy had said once that the window of a stationery store affected her the way a candy shop window affected most girls. She always wanted to put her nose against the glass and study the intriguing array of pencils, notebooks, sharpeners, and paper clips. When she'd been a small girl, one of her favorite games had been " office," and she had never outgrown her fondness for the blank pages of notebooks on which she could scribble.

A hurried ruffling showed her that this notebook was mostly beautiful empty pages, and the old longing to fill them seized her. She certainly had enough to write about now. She would head the book, " Mystery on Mackinac," and put down everything that had happened since she had come here. Perhaps putting it down would help her to find a clue that would lead to some of the answers. Besides, it would be a sort of record of the summer for daddy to read when they returned to Chicago.

It was too bad that someone had already used up a few of the pages, but she could easily tear those out. What neat writing, she thought, as she ripped out the first page. Her journals always seemed to be scrawly, but these letters made a beautiful, orderly pattern across the page.

On the second page the words " Arch Rock " caught her eye. Someone had been writing about the Rock in this very book. Probably Aunt Martha. Words seemed to leap out at her:

"I think J.B. proposed to Sarah on the trip we made to Arch Rock yesterday. I've never seen her behave so absent-mindedly. At her age it is ridiculous. I am sure J.B. would never be the man for her, and, besides, I need her here. Sarah has a serious turn of mind, and she has the responsibility of a daughter to raise. He is much too frivolous for her. The one thing to recommend him is that he knows birds."

Taffy looked up from the book. "J.B." Where had she seen those initials before? And then she remembered. J.B. was the amateur artist who had painted the picture of Aunt Martha surrounded by birds. Sarah must be Donna's mother, and the artist must be the man who had wanted to marry Mrs. Tuckerman.

What had become of him, Taffy wondered. Was he still fond of Mrs. Tuckerman, wherever he was? It was romantic in a way — like something out of a storybook. But she

wanted to put her own words on paper. She folded the torn-out sheets without reading further and put them into an envelope. They might be something her mother would want to look through later. Then she went to work on the beginning of her journal, a project that took up quite a bit of the afternoon.

The Harrisons and Colonel Linwood signed up for the Arch Rock trip, and Mr. and Mrs. Gage signed below them. The list grew. Two schoolteachers from Detroit asked interested questions, and at dinner Taffy was able to report a success.

Tonight she and Donna would be back in their own beds. The window the gull had broken had been repaired, but the Twigs' room stood vacant. Taffy was thankful, as she went up to bed, that tonight she would sleep with two floors between her and the locked room. She felt brave and bold in the daytime, but darkness made a difference. She almost hoped there would be no further opportunity to open the locked door if the opportunity had to come at night. She wasn't sure at all that she could be as brave as David felt *he* would be.

She fell asleep quickly. Perhaps it was the music that awoke her a little later. The upper floor was quiet, but downstairs one of the guests was playing the piano. She listened drowsily.

Moonlight streamed through the window, and a dreamy shadow seemed to keep time to the music. She watched the shadow through half-raised lashes before she came wide awake. Why should there be a moving shadow on the wall?

She sat up in bed, but the moon slipped behind a cloud and the shadow vanished. The window was only a patch of darkness against the night. Then, against the dark window, a darker form appeared, and she heard a faint tapping against the glass.

Her first impulse was to run downstairs. How *could* anything real be outside a third-floor window? The moon came from behind the cloud, the window began to silver with light, and the night outside grew brighter. The sound ceased, and Taffy thought the thing — whatever it was — had gone. Then a dark shape brushed past the pane, and she saw the contour of a wing in the moonlight.

Why, it was only another bird out there in the night! That was strange, but not frightening.

Taffy ran her feet into slippers and put on her robe, her eyes fixed on the window. But apparently the bird had flown away. She leaned her elbows on the sill and looked out into the quiet, moon-bathed yard of the hotel.

She was about to get back into bed when a door in the corridor opened and a woman's voice called: "Oh, do please come, somebody! There's a big bird trying to get in my window!"

Taffy recognized the voice of one of the Detroit teachers and hurried into the hall. Apparently her mother had been coming upstairs with Mrs. Tuckerman because they were there ahead of her. The piano-playing downstairs went on without interruption, and only one door on the corridor opened. That was Mr. Gage's.

"Must be the same bird that tried to get in my window," he said. "I waved a towel, but it was a nervy thing — took a lot to discourage it."

Taffy followed her mother and Mrs. Tuckerman to the room, but there was no bird at the window, no rustling, no tapping against the pane.

Mrs. Tuckerman was trying to reassure the teacher. "Miss Irwin always fed the gulls," she explained, "and they still come back. Though I don't think one has ever tried to get into the house."

Taffy left the room and found her way downstairs to the first floor. For some reason she felt an urgent need to know if Aunt Martha's office was empty and the door to the room still locked.

The guests in the lounge had apparently heard nothing of what had happened upstairs. Taffy went quietly through to the door of the office. There she stopped in surprise.

Before the strange bird picture of Aunt Martha stood a man completely absorbed in the painting. There was no mistaking that short, round figure, and the little fringe of hair about the bald head.

"Hello, Mr. Bogardus," Taffy said.

He turned, and in that second something clicked in Taffy's mind. Those initials in the corner of the picture were "J.B." J.B. for Jeremiah Bogardus?

Of course. And that meant that Mr. Bogardus was the artist who had painted the picture. That also meant he was the man in Aunt Martha's journal — the man who had proposed to Sarah Tuckerman at Arch Rock. She plunged into words without stopping to think about their possible wisdom.

"Some people moved out today," she said breathlessly. "If you still want a room at Sunset House, you can have one. I can check you in right away."

CHAPTER
⤜ 14 ⤛

Spirit Feathers

MR. BOGARDUS beamed. "Well, this is an unexpected windfall. Are you sure it would be all right. I mean — "

"Oh, of course!" Taffy suddenly wasn't as confident as she sounded, but she wanted to get him safely checked in before Mrs. Tuckerman came downstairs. Why the housekeeper had not wanted him here she couldn't understand. But once he was checked in, perhaps she wouldn't really mind and everything would be fixed up.

She went into the hall to the cabinet where the register was kept and put it on a table for him to sign. Mr. Bogardus made no comment about the odd fact that she was downstairs at this hour in pajamas and bathrobe, but he did ask, hesitantly, if it wouldn't be better to have Mrs. Tuckerman or her mother check him in.

"They're busy upstairs," Taffy told him hastily. "A bird of some kind — a sea gull, I guess — has been flying around the windows. One of the ladies got scared, but of course that was silly."

"A sea gull?" Mr. Bogardus echoed.

Taffy decided to get away from the subject of queer happenings at Sunset House. "Day after tomorrow the *Voyageurs* Club is going to have a conducted trip to Arch Rock. Everybody at the hotel is invited. We're going to take lunches. Would you like to go?"

"Sounds good," Mr. Bogardus said. "Just what is the *Voyageurs* Club?"

"It's something David Marsh and I made up today," Taffy explained. "Donna Tuckerman and Henry Fox are in it too. Henry Fox is going to be our Indian guide."

"Better and better." Mr. Bogardus smiled. "Arch Rock is one of my favorite spots on the island."

He looked a little wistful, and Taffy remembered again what she had read in Aunt Martha's journal. Then his eyes seemed to look beyond her and to brighten. Taffy, glancing back over her shoulder, saw Mrs. Tuckerman standing on the bottom step of the stairs.

"We had a room this time," Taffy said breathlessly.

The housekeeper looked from Taffy to Mr. Bogardus and back to Taffy again. "Really!" she said. "After this, Taffy, it might be better if you call your mother or me when a guest wants a room."

Mr. Bogardus was plainly embarrassed. "I'm sorry, Sarah. If you'd rather I didn't take the room —"

And then something unexpected happened. Donna Tuckerman, also clad in pajamas and a robe, came down behind her mother. She hesitated for a moment and then flung herself down the stairs and into Mr. Bogardus' arms.

"Uncle Jerry!" she cried. "Oh, Uncle Jerry, I'm glad you've come back!"

Mr. Bogardus let Donna nearly strangle him with her hug.

"Donna!" There was something strange in Mrs. Tuckerman's voice. "You shouldn't be downstairs. Please go back to bed at once."

Reluctantly Donna went upstairs past her mother and past Mrs. Saunders, who had just started down. Taffy sighed her relief. This was one time when she felt she needed mother badly.

And then she received another surprise.

"Uncle Jerry!" her mother cried, sounding almost like Donna. "Do you remember me? You were my favorite person at Sunset House all one summer when I was in my teens. I'm Miss Irwin's niece, Betty."

Taffy thought for a moment that her mother would imitate Donna and fling her arms about Mr. Bogardus' neck, but evidently she remembered just in time that she was grown up and shook his hand warmly.

"Do you know Jeremiah Bogardus?" she asked Mrs. Tuckerman.

Mrs. Tuckerman's cheeks were pink. "Of course," she said a little stiffly.

What was the matter with her, Taffy wondered. At one time she must have liked Mr. Bogardus a lot, yet she had refused him a room and seemed actually displeased that he was now a guest. Without guests what would happen to Sunset House? Or was it that — a thought began to take root in Taffy's mind.

"I have suggested to Taffy," Mrs. Tuckerman said, "that it would be wiser to call one of us when a guest desires a room."

"But there was nobody here!" Taffy protested. "Mr. Bogardus wanted a room a couple of days ago, but Mrs. Tuckerman told him there weren't any empty. The Twigs' room is empty now and —"

Mrs. Saunders stopped the flow of words. "I'm sure there must have been some misunderstanding, Uncle Jerry. We'd love to have you. And, Taffy, Mrs. Tuckerman is right. When there is hotel business to transact, the thing to do is to call one of us."

Taffy felt suddenly resentful and angry. "I don't think she *wants* people to come to Sunset House! I don't think —"

"Taffy!" Mrs. Saunders' tone carried a quality Taffy could not ignore. "You shouldn't be downstairs at this hour. Go up to bed at once. But first tell Mrs. Tuckerman you are sorry for your rudeness."

Taffy mumbled an apology and started upstairs unhappily. She got into bed feeling that the world was against her and life was full of injustice. She wished miserably that her father were here. Daddy would never have treated her like this. She had only wanted to help open her mother's eyes to what Mrs. Tuckerman was really like.

But underneath her dejection and longing for her father, a persistent voice managed to make itself heard.

" You *were* rude," it said. " Your father wouldn't stand up for you now and you know it. Besides, are you sure you're right about Mrs. Tuckerman? If somebody like Mr. Bogardus likes her, then maybe she's really nice."

She turned her head from side to side, trying to shake the voice into silence. It was getting her all mixed up and she didn't know what to think.

She snuggled beneath the covers, determined to go to sleep quickly. There was always the chance that tomorrow would be better than today. In the morning she meant to get away early and go up to David's. She would tell him about these new developments and see what he thought of them.

In the last moment before falling asleep she wondered drowsily about the bird at the window, which she had almost forgotten in the excitement of checking Mr. Bogardus into a room. *Had* it been a sea gull? And why was it so persistent about trying to get in through a Sunset House window? Had Grayfeather escaped? Had the baby gull come flying back to the hotel because here it had been treated well? This was another thing she'd have to check tomorrow.

But long before she saw David the following morning, she saw Celeste. She awoke early, before her mother was up. Looking out of the window of her room, she saw the cook sitting on her favorite rock beside the water. Taffy skimped on her hair-combing and face-washing and flew downstairs to the garden.

"Did you find out anything about that key?" she asked eagerly the moment she reached Celeste's side.

Celeste had a way of ignoring questions and going off on some track of her own. "I knew something had got out of that room," she said, watching the gulls wheel over the water. "I've heard about that winged thing at the window last night."

"It was only a sea gull," Taffy said. "I saw it."

Celeste nodded. "But it was not a live one like the one that came in during the storm. It was a spirit bird, out of a room that should never have been opened."

"Oh, Celeste," Taffy protested, "that's silly!"

The woman's dark eyes were somber. There was something about her look, Taffy thought, that was positively spooky. Were there, on old, old Mackinac, such strange things as spirit birds? She remembered the moment she had stood on the dark threshold of the locked room. She remembered the silver-gray feather she had found caught in the door. She felt for it now, drew it from her pocket, and held it out.

"Is this a spirit feather, Celeste?"

Celeste drew away and would not touch it. "Where did you get that?"

"It was caught in the door of the locked room. But I shouldn't think you could hold a spirit feather in your hand. Here, feel it; it's real." She reached out and brushed the softness of the feather down the woman's arm.

Celeste shrank back as if the touch had been fire. "Throw it out to the wind!" she cried. "Hold it on your hand and let the wind take it! Quickly, quickly, before much harm is done!"

In spite of her disbelief in spirit birds and spirit feathers a startled Taffy hastened to obey. The breeze lifted the feather and carried it over the water. Then, as if tired of its plaything, the breeze dropped the delicate tuft, and Taffy saw it bob and drift with the small waves.

"One of them has escaped," Celeste brooded. "It is as I thought."

Spookiness couldn't live long in bright, early-morning sunshine. Good sense came back to Taffy. "That wasn't a spirit gull," she said stoutly. "A spirit bird wouldn't brush against a window so that you could hear it. You know what I think? I think it was Grayfeather."

Celeste's look was hard and suspicious. "What is this Grayfeather?"

"I mean the baby gull we rescued during the storm. Henry and Donna put it out to fly away, but it couldn't fly, so I took it up to David Marsh's house. He's going to keep it till it gets well."

"You think it escaped and came back to the hotel last night?"

Taffy hesitated. "I don't know for sure, but it might have. I'm going up to David's after breakfast and find out. That is, if there's going to be any breakfast. Aren't you working today, Celeste?"

Celeste shook her head. "So far I have not decided. It is foolish to cook for guests who will leave anyway. The spirits have doomed Sunset House."

"But I tell you it was a *real* gull, Celeste. I'm sure it was."

Just then someone came out on the veranda and down the rear steps, stepping along jauntily with his shoulders back.

Taffy sighed. "I expect Mr. Bogardus is hungry. Oh, Celeste, couldn't you —"

"Who did you say?" Celeste demanded quickly.

"Mr. Bogardus. He's one of the new guests."

To her amazement, Celeste sprang up from the rock and started across the lawn. Mr. Bogardus, in turn, came toward her with his hand outstretched. This, apparently, was to be another like yesterday's happy greetings. *Everyone* knew Mr. Bogardus!

"Celeste!" he cried. "It's good to see you again. How hungry I am for one of your good breakfasts! Wheat cakes, perhaps, with little pig sausages. And that coffee that nobody can make like Celeste Cloutier."

Celeste was transformed. "It is time you came home to this place," she told him. "The little one needs you. And the older one too, if only she would be wise. Such a breakfast you shall have! It is already on the way. A cook needs the inspiration of someone who appreciates food."

Off she went toward the kitchen, still prophesying what a breakfast this would be. Spirit birds and spirit feathers had been forgotten.

"Hello, Mr. Bogardus," Taffy said. "It's a good thing she saw you. She was getting difficult again."

He gave her his special smile. "Do you have to call me 'Mr. Bogardus'? I'm Uncle Jerry to your mother, so I don't see why I can't be Uncle Jerry to you."

"O. K., Uncle Jerry," Taffy said happily. "Maybe you can sit at our table. Donna would like that."

"So would I," said Uncle Jerry.

By the time Mrs. Tuckerman came into the dining room to breakfast, Uncle Jerry was seated at the table and there was not a thing she could do about it.

CHAPTER
❧ 15 ❧
The Chinese Gong

AFTER breakfast Taffy went up the hill to David's. As she climbed the heights she found herself remembering that day on the lake boat when the high green island of Mackinac had risen from the water. It had seemed then that the island was promising her something — something exciting, something mysterious, that would be like nothing that had happened to her before. And strange things *had* been happening ever since she had arrived at Sunset House.

She walked through the goblin wood without fear. After the open door and the darkness of the locked room, no mere grove of gloomy trees could upset her.

David came to the door when she rang.

"Do you still have Grayfeather?" she asked breathlessly. "Where do you keep him? Could he get away?"

"Sure, I have him," David said. "He's getting along fine. And you know what? He likes sardines. Come on; I'll show you."

Around at the rear of the house David had built an open shelter for the gull with a dishpan of water sunk into the ground for a pond. The bird was not tethered. He could fly away if he wanted to.

David knelt on the grass and took a sardine from the tin. "I don't think he's well yet. Maybe he's a little afraid to fly until he's strong again."

Grayfeather came over without fear and snatched the sardine from David's fingers.

"Do you suppose he's fooling you?" Taffy speculated. "I mean about flying? Maybe he flies away at night and comes back."

"Could be," David said. "But I don't think so."

Taffy, kneeling, crooned gently as she'd crooned when she'd picked the gull up after his fall from the veranda railing. He cocked his head and seemed to listen. He didn't mind when she reached out to stroke his feathers.

"Let's try something, David. Let's find out whether he can fly. Put him on a low branch."

David picked Grayfeather up with hands as gentle as Henry's and carried him to a nearby tree. The bird fluttered and clung to the roost.

"Now, then," Taffy directed, "hold a sardine out to him."

David caught the idea. He walked toward Grayfeather's perch, his hand extended, his fingers holding a sardine temptingly. The gull reached out with his bill, but David stepped out of reach. Taffy could see how much Grayfeather wanted the sardine. He perked his head on this side and then on that and fluttered his beautiful silvergray wings. But he did not leave his perch.

"I guess you're right." Taffy sighed. "I don't think he's ready to fly. I wish he was our suspect, but he can't be."

"A suspect for what?"

"A sea gull tried to get in the windows of Sunset House last night. I saw him at our window, and he tried a couple of others and frightened some of the guests. Sometimes I think grownups are sort of silly about the things that scare them."

David agreed. "I know; it's just like grandmother. She doesn't think I ought to listen to thrillers on the radio. But she's the one they really scare."

"Anyway," Taffy said, "I thought it might be Grayfeather coming back for a visit. But I guess he's still afraid to fly."

Perhaps Grayfeather heard and understood and was a little indignant. He took off from the roost with a great flutter of wings, flew in a circle about the garden, and swooped down to perch on David's shoulder. Taffy squealed in excitement, and David winced as the gull's claws gripped through his thin shirt.

"He wants another sardine!" Taffy cried. "He showed us he can fly, so now you're supposed to reward him."

David held another sardine up within reach and Grayfeather took it greedily.

"That's all," David told the gull, and set him down near the pan of water. "I guess we have our answer, Taffy. If he can fly when he wants to, maybe he did fly down to the hotel last night."

"I know how we can check it for sure," Taffy said. "Maybe tonight you could fasten him by one foot. Do you think that would be too mean?"

"Not just for once," David told her. "We have to remember he's wild and ought to fly back to his own kind. But tonight I'll fasten him, and then if a bird comes around the hotel it won't be Grayfeather. What I don't see is why it's so important."

"It's important because of Celeste," Taffy explained. "If we can prove it's Grayfeather, she'll stop talking about spirit birds."

As they walked back to the house and sat on the front steps, Taffy told David of her conversation with Celeste that morning, about checking Mr. Bogardus into the hotel and finding that just about everybody at Sunset House knew him and liked him. Everybody, that is, except Mrs. Tuckerman. She told about the J.B. painting, and about what Aunt Martha had written in her journal.

"I wonder why Mr. Bogardus is so anxious to stay at Sunset House?" she finished. "I wonder if he could be here for some special purpose? Of course," she added hastily, "it would be a good purpose."

David wasn't so sure. "They use that trick in mysteries. They make the person who seems awfully nice turn out in the end to be the murderer."

"There isn't any murderer at Sunset House," Taffy said coldly, "but I see what you mean. I told you Mrs. Tuckerman thinks the secret part of the will might leave the hotel to some bird society if mother doesn't get it. If Mr. Bogardus is mixed up with birds, do you suppose he could represent the society?"

David thought it over. "If that's right, he might want to see things go wrong at the hotel so that it would come to the society. That would be a motive. You always have to have a motive. But there has to be an opportunity to commit the crimes too. How could Mr. Bogardus put a bat skeleton in Miss Twig's bed, or open the locked door? He hasn't been inside the hotel until now."

"Then that lets him out!" Taffy agreed in relief. "I wouldn't *really* suspect him of anything. Maybe it's just Mrs. Tuckerman that interests him at the hotel. Donna's crazy about him; I think she'd like it if her mother married him. But Mrs. Tuckerman seemed upset when Donna was glad to see him."

No matter how they tried they couldn't figure any of it out.

In the afternoon, back at the hotel, Taffy discovered a croquet set in the storeroom. She and Donna set out the wickets. Uncle Jerry Bogardus joined them on the lawn and, when David dropped in at just the right time, they arranged a team match — Uncle Jerry and Donna against David and Taffy.

David and Taffy won most of the games. Donna was an

expert, but Uncle Jerry's balls were always turning up miles from the wicket he was trying for. He said it really wasn't fair for Donna to play under the handicap of such a partner, but Donna wouldn't give him up.

Once they even tried to get Henry Fox to play, but he said he was too busy with his work in the garden, though now and then Taffy saw him watching the players and

smiling over one of Uncle Jerry's jokes. Apparently Henry also liked Mr. Bogardus.

While resting after the game, Donna mentioned the gong.

"You gave it to Miss Irwin, didn't you, Uncle Jerry?" she asked.

Mr. Bogardus mopped his glowing pink face. "That's right, honey. I picked it up in China, in a little shop in Shanghai."

"I rang it yesterday," Taffy said. "I didn't know such a little gong could have such a big voice."

"It has a big voice all right," Uncle Jerry said. "Did I ever tell you the story about it, Donna?"

"Tell it now!" Donna cried. "I love your stories."

Mr. Bogardus chuckled. You knew that he liked children, Taffy thought, and he would never, never do anything to hurt anyone, not even if he really did represent a bird society and want the hotel to go to the birds.

"A long time ago," Uncle Jerry began, "before any of you were born, that gong hung in a temple on a hillside above the Yangtze River. It bonged at sunset every night for the temple ceremonies and it bonged at sunrise to wake up the little valley town. The people of the town said its golden voice spoke of good things — of growing rice crops, and words sung by the great poets of China, and brush strokes of black ink taking beautiful form on white rice paper.

"But sometimes the gong whispered in strange ways and at strange hours when no priests were near it. Though it was only a whisper of sound, it could be heard through the quiet valley, like the brushing of wings against the bronze."

Wings again! Taffy thought. Did everything at Sunset House have to end with wings?

"Neither the valley people nor the temple priests were upset when this happened. When the golden whisper went out over the valley, they said to themselves, 'It is our Winged Lady of the mountaintops watching over us and wishing us well.' And they went about their work undisturbed.

"Then one night a storm came down from the mountains and the great River of Golden Sands began to rise. As the yellow waters poured across the fields, a great crashing sound echoed over the hills and through the valley, a sound that was louder than the storm. The people rushed out of their homes and, seeing the danger, climbed to the safety of high places. Even though many of them lost their meager possessions, their lives and the lives of those they loved were saved from the rushing waters."

"And it was the gong?" Donna asked. "It was the Winged Lady?"

"So people said. The priests were sleeping and would never have roused the people. But the warning of the gong woke them and led them to safety."

"How did *you* get the gong?" David asked, practical as always. "Didn't the people of the valley want to keep it?"

"I'm sure they wanted to," Mr. Bogardus said sadly, "but wars came to China and the armies of the north fought the armies of the south. The temple on the hill was destroyed. The gong would have been destroyed too, if one of the priests hadn't escaped and taken it with him.

"He tried to reach the city, but sickness and hunger made him weak, and he died soon after he arrived at the home of friends. His friends knew the story of the gong, but they were poor and it could be sold for food. So it found its way into a shop in Shanghai. That was where I found it years ago and bought it."

They all liked the story. Henry had stopped work to listen, and down at the end of the veranda Celeste leaned upon the rail. Taffy had an idea this was the sort of story Celeste would like, for though it came from so far away a country as China it was something akin to the legends of Mackinac Island. It was the kind of story Celeste would believe.

The golden voice of the gong rang the dinner summons and the party broke up. As Taffy passed the dining-room door she reached out and touched the cool bronze of the gong wonderingly. How did it like being here? Did it mind that its only duty now was to call people to dinner? Did it miss the mysterious wings that had sometimes brushed its surface? It was only a story, of course. But Mr. Bogardus had made it so real that the gong seemed like a personage to whom she ought to pay the greatest respect.

CHAPTER

❧ 16 ❦

On Manito Trail

THAT night Taffy slept peacefully, right through till morning. But when she went down to breakfast, she learned that the disturbing gull had again visited Sunset House.

Mother was in the hallway, at the foot of the stairs, talking to the Detroit schoolteachers whose bags stood beside them. Mr. Gage was grumpily joining in their complaints.

The bird had been flapping around the windows, behaving very queerly indeed. It would swoop past, brush the pane with its wings, turn somewhere in the darkness, and wheel back. Sometimes it struck the glass with its beak.

"We simply can't stand another night of this," one of the teachers was saying. "It's too upsetting." They liked Sunset House, they assured Mrs. Saunders, and had hoped to stay for several more weeks. But now they felt there was nothing to do but move to a hotel not quite so popular with sea gulls.

Mr. Gage had seen the bird at his window, but had pulled the shade down. He was annoyed.

"No bird in its right mind would act like that," he sputtered. "You'd better take steps to get rid of the thing. Trap it, or shoot it, or do something about it."

Taffy listened in dismay. Had David forgotten his promise to fasten Grayfeather? Had the gull escaped and come back to the hotel for a second night? If not, had

someone put food out on the window sills to attract a gull?
But if that had happened, why was there only one gull?
Why hadn't several of them come screaming in to fight
for the food as they usually did?

Mrs. Saunders watched unhappily as the teachers left
and Mr. Gage and his wife went in to breakfast.

"I don't know what to do," she told Taffy. "How *do*
you get rid of a persistent sea gull? If this keeps up, and
people are disturbed every night, we shan't have any
guests left."

When Doris brought in breakfast, she was worried too.

"Celeste is getting us all jittery," she complained to
Taffy, "saying it's a spirit bird and that it means bad luck
for anyone who sees it. Some of the girls are talking of
quitting."

"*I* saw it and I haven't had any bad luck," Taffy pointed
out. "You don't believe in spirit birds, do you?"

Doris shook her head. "I don't, but I hope your mother
and Mrs. Tuckerman can do something about it."

Later, while waiting on the veranda for the *Voyageurs*
to start, Taffy spoke to Mr. Bogardus about the gull.

Uncle Jerry looked oddly thoughtful. "I've met a few
birds in my life, but I've never known a gull that acted
like this one."

"It could be a baby gull, couldn't it?" Taffy asked. "I
mean one that was a little tame and knew its way to the
hotel?"

"I doubt it," Uncle Jerry said.

When David arrived, Taffy found out that last night's
gull couldn't have been Grayfeather. David had fastened
their gull securely, and it had still been tethered in the
morning. About that David was positive.

Celeste had packed wonderful lunch boxes. Taffy had a
suspicion that that was because Mr. Bogardus was going
on the trip. Eight of the guests had registered, and the

start was scheduled for nine thirty. Henry Fox, very neat in khaki trousers and shirt, came out on the porch looking authentically Indian, even if he didn't wear feathers.

" Everybody ready? " he asked, and started down the porch steps. But before the others could follow him, a slight little woman in black, carrying a suitcase, came up the driveway to the hotel.

" Hello, Taffy! " she called. " I've come back."

It was Miss Hattie Twig. Taffy ran to help with her suitcase.

" You mean you're coming back to Sunset House? " Taffy asked.

" That's right. I like it here."

Taffy felt like hugging her. " I'll run and tell mother. Maybe you'd like to come on our trip this morning."

The *Voyageurs* agreed to wait for Miss Hattie to join them. It developed that she knew Mr. Bogardus, but having everybody know Uncle Jerry was no longer a surprise to Taffy.

Once the party had started off, Henry proved to be surprisingly talkative, and readily answered questions about the old trails they followed. Reaching the heights, they cut into deep woods, and the party stretched out in single file. Taffy had been a little afraid she would have to look out for Miss Hattie, but Mr. Bogardus gallantly took on the task of helping her.

When they came to a clearing in the trees and paused to rest, Henry told them about the way they had come.

" We've been following Manito Trail," he said. " Gitchie Manito was the Algonquins' Great Spirit, but there were lots of other spirits too. Some good and some bad."

" Could people see them? " Taffy asked curiously.

" Only when they took the shape of some animal, or bird, or reptile. You were supposed to be able to tell between the good and the bad. The bad one would be twisted or misshapen in some way. Or it would do something that the real animal, or bird, would never do."

Mrs. Harrison looked amused, but Mrs. Gage, who usually let her husband do the talking, spoke up timidly. "That gull at the window! Perhaps that's a manito."

"Celeste says it's a spirit bird," Donna put in. "A bad spirit."

There was an uncomfortable pause, and then, once more, Taffy could have hugged Miss Hattie.

"What fun!" she cried. "Where else in the world could you meet an old Indian spirit? Oh, I *do* hope the gull comes to my window tonight."

Someone laughed and the awkward moment was gone. Even Mr. Gage gave a rumble of laughter from deep down in his throat. But to Taffy's surprise Uncle Jerry, who usually laughed so easily, was not laughing at all.

When they started off again, Taffy dropped back so that she could walk with Uncle Jerry and Miss Hattie.

"Do you belong to any kind of bird society, Uncle Jerry?" she asked.

He looked a little surprised. "Why, yes, I do. I've always been interested in birds. In fact, that's how I happened to meet Miss Irwin years ago. We became acquainted at a meeting of our national bird society. The following summer I came to Sunset House for the first time."

"Do you think if my mother doesn't make a success of the hotel it will go to the birds?"

"Go to — oh, you mean to the society?" Mr. Bogardus looked really surprised this time. "Why do you think that?"

"Donna says that's what her mother thinks, but Celeste thinks the hotel will go to Mrs. Tuckerman."

Mr. Bogardus pursed his lips. "There's no telling what whim might have seized Martha Irwin. She was a very strong-minded woman."

" I know how you could find out," Miss Twig said un-expectedly. " Miss Irwin kept journals and told them everything. Several times she read us passages from them, and they were always interesting. If she made plans, she put them in the journals. If you can find the right one — "

" I did find one! " Taffy cried. " But it had only a few written pages in it, and I tore them out. I'll look again when we get back to the hotel."

Up ahead the leaders of the party were disappearing around a bend in the trail.

" Anyway," Taffy announced resolutely, " it doesn't mat-ter who's supposed to get Sunset House if mother fails, because she isn't going to fail."

" Then what will happen? " Uncle Jerry asked, as they hurried after the rest of the party.

" Why, mother will sell it, of course, so we can get a house of our own in Chicago." Like the turning of an electric switch, a flash of inspiration went through her. " So m-m-maybe — " she began to stammer with eager-ness, " maybe *you* could buy it, Uncle Jerry."

He smiled at her cheerfully. " How did you guess that I had something like that in mind? "

Of course, Taffy thought. That was why Uncle Jerry was at Sunset House. It made more sense than a bird society. Now there was a buyer waiting, and everything would work out fine — if they could only get rid of the silly gull that was disturbing the guests.

They quickened their pace. The party had stopped above the steep, rocky drop of Robinson's Folly, and Henry was telling the story of the precipice.

" It was named for Captain Daniel Robertson, but the way the French said it made it sound like Robinson, so that's what they call it today. He was in love with a Chip-pewa girl, whose father had been a chief under the great Pontiac and hated all white men.

"The girl's father wanted her to marry a man of her own tribe, but the captain stole the girl away and built a house for her on the cliff. The Indian who had wanted to marry her found her there and killed her; then he and Captain Robertson had a terrible fight and both fell over the cliff."

Taffy looked over the dizzy drop and drew back with a shudder.

Now the trail wound along the face of the steep hill. Sometimes the woods thinned, and Taffy caught a glimpse of water far below. The path ended in a turn-around clearing for carriages. At one side were low, shedlike buildings where soda pop and souvenirs were sold.

"Gimcracks and pop in a place like this!" Mr. Gage snorted. But Donna and David and Taffy discovered they were enormously thirsty and blissfully sucked ice-cold liquid through a straw.

Ahead of them rose the great arch. Taffy looked down through an almost perfect circle of rock to the trees and cliff below, and the bright, sunny blue of Lake Huron.

"It must have been here an awfully long while," she said softly as Henry came to stand beside her. "Thousands of years, maybe."

"Since the beginning of time." Henry's voice was low. "My people say this was the gateway through which the Great Spirit came to Mackinac. He stood upon the highest point of the arch and raised his arms in blessing over Michilimackinac. There's another legend too about the arch."

"Tell me," Taffy said.

"The story goes that it was carved by the tears of the maiden, Red Wing, who wept for her star lover until the rock crumbled and the light of the evening star came through."

"I like that," Taffy said. And suddenly she wanted more

than anything else to be friends with this Indian boy. Perhaps if he knew she had taken care of the gull, he might
like her better.

She began a little hesitantly. "You know the gull that
came through the window in the storm? Well, it wasn't
strong enough to fly away again. I put it back in the hatbox and took it up to David's. We've named it Grayfeather."

She gave Henry a quick, sidelong glance and saw that
he was staring at the arch, a faraway look in his eyes. She
couldn't be sure he had heard her.

Behind them Mr. Gage spoke to his wife. "The arch is
limestone," he said. "It was one of the first points to
emerge from the water in the days when Mackinac was
part of the lake bottom. The waves wore away the soft
parts of the rock and left the arch standing when the water
receded."

Taffy liked Henry's stories better, especially the story
about Red Wing and the evening star. She climbed to the
raised platform leading to the base of the natural bridge
and joined David and Miss Hattie. Far below she saw
bright pebbles in the clear depth of the water. Her eyes
came back to the arch.

"You know what *I'd* like to do?" she said. "I'd like to
walk across it."

"That's not allowed," David said. "The rock's too crum-
bly, and if you fell, you'd be killed. People used to cross
over a long time ago when it was stronger."

Taffy thought Henry had remained with the Gages. She
was surprised to feel him brush past her and go lightly up
the narrow, arched bridge, his moccasins firm on the rock.
At the highest point of the arch he stopped and stood
there perfectly balanced, looking out over the water, a
proud smile on his lips.

One of the women gave a suppressed cry, and Colonel

Linwood shouted: "You! Boy! Come down from there!"

Henry did not turn his head at the shout. He seemed, Taffy thought, to be a part of that wild place, and suddenly she understood. He wasn't showing off. His people had belonged here long before the white man came, and it was as natural for him to cross that arch as it would be for David to walk upon a white man's bridge. His feet moved so lightly that no stone crumbled beneath their weight. He was one with the trees and the wind and the rocky chasm below.

Uncle Jerry touched Colonel Linwood's arm. "Don't shout at him. He won't fall."

Taffy waited breathlessly. As sure-footed as he had gone up the arch, Henry came down.

Mr. Gage began to sputter. "Of all the hairbrain —"

"It's time for lunch," Henry said calmly. His eyes met Taffy's for a brief, friendly moment.

She was, she thought, the only one who knew why Henry had wanted to go out on the rock, and Henry knew she understood.

Celeste's good lunch was eaten leisurely, but nothing more was said about a boy who had run out upon a perilous arch. Not until shortly before the return to Sunset House did David make a proposal about Henry.

"You know what?" he said. "Henry's done such a good job of playing guide this trip that I think he ought to have a feather to wear like the leaders of those old *voyageurs*. I brought one along, just in case."

The feather was silver, like the one Taffy had found caught in the door. Only this one, she was sure, had been contributed by Grayfeather and not by any mysterious spirit bird.

"Since you're not wearing a hat, Henry," Uncle Jerry said, "you can put it through a buttonhole in your shirt."

Henry looked embarrassed as he took the feather, and

did not put it in a buttonhole as Uncle Jerry had suggested. Instead, he gave it to Donna, and the girl laughed and stuck it through her dark curls.

Why hadn't he wanted to wear it, Taffy wondered. With all those legends he knew about Mackinac, did he, like Celeste, believe in the manito? Did he believe, perhaps, that a gull could be a bad manito come to plague the people of Sunset House? She shook the idea aside almost as quickly as it came. Henry was too sensible. Probably he just thought the feather idea silly.

On the return trip, the party left Manito Trail and went down the wider, easier path of Arch Rock Road. David took the lead, the way being easy and the guided part of the trip over. Henry dropped to the rear, and Donna Tuckerman walked beside him.

Once, rounding a curve in the road, Taffy looked back and saw Donna and Henry talking earnestly. Donna looked angry, as though she did not like what Henry was saying, and Henry had an odd, unhappy look in his eyes.

What was that all about, Taffy wondered. Well, there was no use trying to guess. She was glad a direct course of action was open to her when she returned to the hotel. The very first thing she was going to do was look through Aunt Martha Irwin's desk to see if she could find another journal.

CHAPTER 17

Seven Keys

A DISCOURAGED Taffy sat at Aunt Martha's desk. She had searched every drawer in the desk and had poked through the stacks of tied-up magazines. The only result had been a great rousing of dust. Where, where, *where* lay the answer to the mysteries? If it was in the journals, where were the journals? Shut away in the locked room? Was that why the room was locked? In that case, unless she could get into the room, she was stopped.

Frowning, she concentrated on places other than the locked room where Aunt Martha might have stored the journals. There was that cubbyhole storeroom under the rear veranda where she had found the croquet set. But that seemed to be a place for gardening tools and outdoor games. Next, there was the big storeroom on the first floor. She had poked into that once and had found that it held only kitchen supplies, canned goods, stores of flour and sugar, and that sort of thing. On the second floor was a big linen closet, but that too would be no place to store old journals.

Suddenly she thought of the attic. The day she had followed Henry up there in search of a hatbox, it had been piled with all sorts of trunks and boxes. It would be just the place to put away old journals. Unless, of course, the journals hid secrets, safe only in a locked room. Something very valuable to Aunt Martha must be in that room, and it could very well be the journals. But at least the attic was worth a try.

She walked through the lounge with no show of haste. She had discovered from long experience that the minute she was bent on some really important private concern of her own, a grownup would step in and send her on an errand, or tell her to do something else. It was better not to attract attention. She was halfway up the stairs when her mother called to her from the landing above.

" Taffy Saunders! What on earth have you been doing? "

" I — I was just looking through some stacks of old magazines," she said truthfully enough.

" Well, go and wash up right away; I don't want anyone to see you looking like that. And whatever you've been into, I do hope you put it back in place."

" I did," Taffy said, and added, " well — sort of." Maybe the magazines weren't exactly the way she had found them, but they weren't messed up too much.

The moment her mother was out of sight down the stairs, she hurried to her room. Washing up should take only about three seconds.

It took exactly two. Cobwebs and the dirt came off largely on the towel. Oh, dear, Taffy thought, she'd been told about that before, but she *was* in a hurry. What she wanted to do was so terribly important. Why, it might mean the whole future of Sunset House!

No one was in sight in the upper hallway as she tiptoed past the closed door of the Tuckermans' room. The last thing she wanted was for Donna to discover what she was up to. There was no telling where Donna fitted into the picture.

One last quick look around, then she popped through the door to the attic stairway and closed it behind her. The stairs were dim, and the old, musty, shut-in smell of the attic closed upon her. When she had followed Henry up the stairs, she had not been alone. Now the stairs were so quiet that her soft footfalls sounded loudly in her ears.

How far away from the rest of the house this seemed! Isolated — that's what it was — dark and shadowy and isolated. But she must not permit her imagination to run away with her this time. David had said girls were too easily scared. She would show him that she was not. After all, what could be here to frighten her? Just a lot of old trunks and boxes and piled-up cartons.

" Behind which somebody could hide," a voice seemed to whisper in her mind.

" Hush! " said Taffy to the voice. " You can't frighten me."

She looked behind every stack, and into every shadowy corner. There was nothing hiding anywhere. She did not so much as see a mouse, which was a good thing, because a mouse might be a manito.

" Oh, stop it! " said Taffy crossly to herself.

She pulled her imagination up short and gave her attention to the boxes. Where to start? How in all this — " welter " would be the word her mother would use — could she pick out the one box that might contain Aunt Martha's journals?

She tried the lid of an old-fashioned trunk. It stuck, but it was not locked, and after a moment she managed to raise the top. The odor of camphor balls drove her back with a gasp. The top tray of the trunk held folded, old-fashioned dresses. She had not played dress-up for a long while — she was getting too big for that — but these clothes certainly looked tempting.

She sighed a little wistfully as she stood beside the raised lid of the trunk and held a bit of lavender satin between her fingers. Sometimes she wanted to grow up more than anything else in the world — wanted to grow up quickly so she could have all the privileges grown-up

people seemed to have. But at times like this, it almost
hurt to think of not being a little girl any more. Real dolls,
and paper dolls, and dress-up and make-believe were all
things to put behind you when you were nearly thirteen.
But when you still loved those things part of the time,
there was a sort of ache when you realized that soon you
would play with them no more. Lots of the things grownups did seemed awfully dull. Just sitting around, for instance, and talking and not *doing* anything. Maybe she
wouldn't be glad to grow up.

Then she remembered a talk she had had with her
father. She had come home almost in tears one day because a girl at school had told her snootily that she was
too big for paper dolls.

Her father had said: "It's easier growing up than you
think, chicken. When you're too big for paper dolls, you'll
know. You won't care about playing with them any more
because new things will interest you more. You won't
mind when it really happens. So play what you like as
long as you want to. You won't want to *too* long."

Maybe, Taffy thought, Donna and she could dress up
in these wonderful old things sometime. But that was not
what she was here for now. No journals were likely to be
found in this trunk. She let the lid down gently and
walked to a pile of cartons.

The cartons were labeled with black crayon letters, and
her heart began to beat excitedly. Oh, if only Aunt Martha had packed the journals in one of these cardboard
boxes marked with what they held!

Choosing one stack, she began to read the lettering.
"BOOKS." "BOOKS." "BOOKS." The entire stack was
books. The next two stacks were also books. Did journals,
perhaps, come under the heading of "Books"? If that was
the case, she'd have to go through all the cartons.

Why were there so many books here if the locked room

had been lined with shelves of them when mother was a little girl? As Taffy moved among the stacks she began to suspect that Aunt Martha must have moved her entire library up here and used the downstairs room for some other purpose. But *what* other purpose?

Taffy went on to the next stack and the word "JOUR-NALS" practically jumped out at her. She was so eager to get the box down that the whole stack came over toward her like the leaning tower of Pisa and she threw her weight against it just in time to prevent a crash that would have echoed through the house.

When the box was safely on the floor, she knelt beside the treasure breathlessly.

The cord was tied in maddeningly tight knots, but she finally managed to slip it off and open the carton. There they were — the journals Aunt Martha had kept for so many years, each one neatly marked with the year it covered.

The top journal was about birds. Mackinac Island birds, particularly — their varieties, habits, and songs. Taffy wrinkled her nose. Had Aunt Martha given over all the journals to doing her homework in bird study? Or had she been writing a book about birds? Then a passage caught her eye:

"I could have wept over the little thing when they brought it to me. It was a rose-breasted grosbeak — quite lifeless, but undamaged in any outer way by the storm that had killed it. I shall take good care of it. I am becoming so skillful that I can almost bring back life to poor dead wings."

What a strange thing to write, Taffy thought. No one could bring back life to something that was dead. Her eye sped down the page and caught Celeste's name.

"Celeste's head is filled with legends and superstitions. She mistrusts my hummingbird. She says that some of

these poor creatures are manitos and that what I do is
dangerous. There is no arguing with her, so I don't try.
At least she knows they are fond of me and may come to
feel that their fondness for me protects the house."

This was making things worse, not better, Taffy felt.
There was no use sampling the journals here and there,
hit or miss. She had better work out some order in which
to read them. There were so many that it would take
longer than she had thought. It wouldn't be a good idea to
disappear up here for too long at a time if she wanted to
keep what she was doing a secret.

She looked through the box until she found the book
that carried a date preceding the unfinished one in the
desk downstairs. This was where she would begin. Then
she'd read back through the books until she found something that would help her. But even though she knew she
must leave the attic soon, she could not help leafing hurriedly through this book. Again a name sprang out at her
— Sarah Tuckerman. She read the neatly written lines, and
a tingle of excitement went through her. By the best of
good fortune she had found the passage that told her one
of the things she wanted to know. Here was the explana-
tion of what Aunt Martha had done to turn Mrs. Tuckerman against Mr. Bogardus.

"I cannot have him come in and walk off with my
housekeeper under my very nose without so much as con-
sulting me! Besides, I don't trust him. He makes friends
too easily. Everyone, from Celeste to the guests, likes him
at first glance. *I* have never made friends as easily as that.
It seems unnatural.

"Somehow I suspect that it is the hotel he is after. He
knows I mean to leave it to Sarah in my will. If he could
stay around and marry Sarah, that would be fine for him.
He would get everything without its costing him a penny.
I mean to open Sarah's eyes."

Somewhere on the floor below a door slammed and Taffy jumped nervously. She'd better not stay here a minute longer. But she would take this book along and read more of it when she had time.

She began to stack the journals back in the box, but they would not fit in properly and she took them out again to see what was in the way. The obstruction was a small box that had dropped down to the bottom of the carton when she had pulled out the journals. Taffy liked boxes — boxes and bottles. You could do all sorts of things with them. But she had not brought many boxes with her to Mackinac, since her mother felt they would take up too much room in the suitcases. This box would do to start a new collection.

She fished out the little box and found it surprisingly heavy. It rattled with a metallic sound that might be made by coins. She opened it and stared with widening eyes.

The box contained seven keys!

There was just one thought in Taffy's mind. Would one of these keys unlock the mysterious door? She left the carton where she had found it and hurried to the stairs.

Halfway across the big room her eyes, now used to the dimness, caught something she had not seen before. On the floor, not far from the stairs, lay the small, silvery feather of a gull!

She picked it up. What was it doing here? Another spirit feather? she wondered. How in the world could the feather of a sea gull be in the attic? Memory painted a sharp picture of the moment David had given one of the baby gull's feathers to Henry Fox because he had been a fine guide. But Henry had given the feather to Donna, and Donna had put it in her hair.

Had Donna come here? If so, why? What was Donna doing in the attic?

She went quietly down the attic stairs and listened a

moment behind the door at the bottom. She did not want to open the door and walk into Donna or Mrs. Tuckerman. All these mysterious things were beginning to gather a sort of momentum, piling up and adding up as if they were almost ready to go somewhere.

The hallway was deserted. She walked downstairs, meaning to slip into the office and try the seven keys if no one was in the lounge. One of these *had* to be the key. It just *had* to be!

But the lounge brought immediate disappointment, for Donna sat curled up in a chair with a book. She glanced up at the sound of Taffy's step.

" What's the matter? " she asked. " You look awfully queer."

As Donna turned her head, Taffy saw the silver gull's feather bright against her dark hair. She felt in her pocket for the attic feather. It was still there.

" I'm all right," she said, and picked up a magazine as though that was what had brought her to the lounge. With the magazine under her arm she went upstairs to her room. If the feather had been missing from Donna's hair, Taffy would have had a clue to the person who might have been in the attic. The feather in her pocket could not have come from Grayfeather.

She opened the little box again and examined the keys. A couple of them looked as if they might be the right size for the door, but she could not be sure until she tried them. And she could not try them with Donna sitting in the lounge. Or with anybody sitting in the lounge, for that matter.

She put the journal away in her own table drawer, walked to the window, and looked up toward David's house. Should she go up there again and consult him about the newest developments? But except for the discovery of the journals and finding out why Mrs. Tuckerman didn't trust Mr. Bogardus, she had nothing much to tell. If she could get that door open, she'd really have news for David, and she'd have accomplished it by herself.

As she gazed out the window, another inspiration struck her. David had been scornful of her failure to get into the room because she had become frightened. So why not show him? Why not wait till tonight and creep down to the room through the sleeping hotel and try the keys? She would take her flashlight this time, so she needn't worry about the dark. If she got the door open, she could explore the room.

She hugged herself happily. This would show David. Of course it *would* take a little courage. But in broad daylight, with sunshine flooding outside, she felt very courageous indeed.

There was just one little prick of conscience that disturbed her, one small inside voice that tried to be heard.

" Why," said the voice, " don't you go to your mother? You know perfectly well that you ought to take the journal and the keys and the feather to her and let her decide what to do with them."

" Oh, go away! " said Taffy to the voice. She knew what might happen if she took this to mother.

She'd be accused of using her imagination again; she'd be told that she was nosing into things that were none of her business; she'd be asked for goodness' sake to forget about that old rubbish-filled room. Or — and this was even worse — her mother would simply take the keys, try them all, and maybe open the door herself. There wouldn't be anything dramatic, or mysterious, or exciting about that. There'd be no chance to prove her courage to David, and probably the person who was behind these mysterious doings would be warned and would go into hiding.

She was sure her way was better. The voice tried to point out that she had been foolishly sure a few other times in her life, but she would not listen.

The day seemed without end. There was the journal she had brought down from the attic, but she couldn't sit quietly and read about the habits of the red-breasted grosbeak. Finally she took her bicycle out and rode all the way around the island. It was a beautiful ride, the woods on one side, the lapping waves on the other. And it hurried the afternoon along.

The day finally passed, and she found herself tucked into bed, supposedly for the night. She dozed off and slept awhile until her mother came to bed. Then she lay tensely awake, listening to the night sounds outside and to the faint hum of the electric clock on the bureau.

When she was sure it must be practically morning, she sat up in bed, reached for the flashlight she had placed beneath her pillow and sent out a thin beam toward the clock. The hands pointed to almost midnight. In the other bed her mother breathed evenly in deep sleep.

She slipped her legs from beneath the covers and reached for her robe. Then she got out of bed, shivering a little in the night air. When she stepped off the scatter rug beside her bed, the floor felt cold to her bare feet, but she could not risk the slap-slap that slippers would make on the stairs.

The bedroom door creaked faintly when she opened it, but her mother's even breathing did not change.

The hallway was long and shadowy, lighted only by a night light. She tiptoed toward the stairs. Not until she was down the first flight did she realize that something was wrong.

The night light on the second floor was out and, leaning over the banister, she saw that no light burned in the hallway at the foot of the stairs. Had someone forgotten to leave the lights on? Or had mysterious fingers turned them off for some purpose? For an instant she was tempted to run upstairs to the safety and warmth of her bed. But the thought of David's scorn kept her putting one foot before the other on the prickly carpet of the stairway.

She had reached the last landing when a roaring, brassy sound crashed about her, echoing to the very roof.

"Bang-bang-cr-ash-bang-ng-ng!"

Taffy clung to the banister, trembling until the sound stopped. Someone had beaten the Chinese gong with a fury that took all the music out of its voice and substituted a wild, harsh, brassy screaming.

CHAPTER
⚹ 18 ⚹
Chief Suspect

TAFFY turned on her flashlight, but its beam showed no one near the gong. Whoever had struck was already gone. She ran down the last flight, and her foot, as she left the bottom step, came down upon something that rolled sickeningly. Her ankle twisted and she fell. Grasping uncertainly, she picked up the thing that had thrown her.

Doors opened on the floors above. A voice called, "What's going on down there?"

Taffy tried to find her voice, to call to them to come down quickly, but brought forth only a quivery whisper. Between the startling clamor of the gong and the shock of her fall, she was too shaken to speak. They were coming anyway, pulling on robes or coats as they came, hurrying and jostling.

Someone turned on the light on the second floor, and in its glow Taffy saw Mr. Gage. After him trooped her mother and Mrs. Tuckerman, Mr. Bogardus, Miss Twig, the Harrisons, Colonel Linwood, and the others. Mr. Gage turned on the hall light, and Taffy experienced a hysterical urge to laugh because everyone looked so funny. Mrs. Tuckerman had cold cream on her face, Miss Twig's hair was up in wire curlers, everyone was wide-eyed with alarm.

There was an odd silence. Taffy saw they were all staring at what she held in her hand. For the first time she looked at the thing she had stepped on. A gaudy, paint-

streaked face grinned at her from the head of the Indian
war club that had hung above the dining-room table.

Her mother slipped down the stairs past the others and
put an arm about her shoulder. "Honey! what is it? What
happened?"

Taffy shook her head helplessly. She could only whisper.
"I don't know. I was coming down the stairs and all of a
sudden the gong began to bang."

Mr. Gage was looking at her suspiciously. He took the
war club from her hand and turned it about.

"The paint's chipped on the head. It was obviously used
to strike the gong."

Taffy recovered her voice abruptly. "But *I* wasn't the
one who used it. I wasn't anywhere near it when it started
that awful banging."

Mr. Bogardus, looking funny and fat in a red-and-white

striped bathrobe, spoke from the stairs.

"Let's look for the one who did ring it. Suppose I search the dining room, while you look in the kitchen, Mr. Gage. Perhaps someone else will search the lounge. The rest of you can stay here so that nobody can go up or down the stairs and slip away."

A voice, heavy and brooding, fell upon the group.

"A search is useless. You will find no one."

Taffy saw Celeste on the upper landing. The cook wore a maroon-colored robe, and her heavy, dark braids hung down the front of it on each side.

"No human hands struck the gong," she went on. "There is a spirit that belonged to it in China. The wings are still there to warn us of danger."

"Poppycock!" snapped Mr. Gage. "Come along, Bogardus. Let's get on with the search. Unless he's escaped outside, whoever rang it is still in the hotel."

While the guests broke up to search the lower floor of the hotel, Mrs. Saunders dropped limply into a chair in the lounge. "Goodness, that gave me a fright! What can possibly be back of such an action? Why would anyone want to startle us out of our beds?"

Mrs. Tuckerman had come into the lounge, shaking her head. "Things like this have never happened here before." She was pale.

Taffy wondered if Mrs. Tuckerman, like Mr. Gage, might think she had rung the gong. She hoped the searchers would come back quickly with whoever must be hiding on the lower floor. Surely it was nobody from the hotel. All the guests could be accounted for.

Donna had followed her mother sleepily. Doris and the other waitresses trailed into sight and hovered behind the guests. Henry Fox came quietly downstairs and joined the searchers as they moved from room to room. There was no one, Taffy thought, to suspect. No one, perhaps, except the Winged Lady of Mr. Bogardus' story.

In a little while the searchers returned.

"We've hunted in every corner," Mr. Bogardus said. "All the windows and doors are locked from the inside, and the door to the back stairway is locked. If the person who rang the gong went out through a window or door, he would have had to leave it open behind him."

"Perhaps someone rushed upstairs past Taffy before the lights were turned on," Miss Twig suggested helpfully.

"Could that be it, Taffy?" Mrs. Saunders asked. "Do you think someone went past you in the dark?"

Taffy could only shake her head. "No one went past me. I had my flashlight on as soon as the gong sounded. If anyone had come up the stairs, I'd have seen him."

"That settles that idea," Mr. Gage glowered. "And it settles something else. My wife and I are leaving tomorrow. I want to sleep through the night without being annoyed by sea gulls and gongs."

Mr. Bogardus crossed the lounge, went into the office, and tried the door to what had been Miss Irwin's library.

"Locked," he said. "Nobody in there."

For just a second Taffy thought she might offer him her keys, and then changed her mind. All of those David called "the suspects" were right in plain sight and had all come downstairs from the upper floors.

Taffy checked them over again in her mind. Sleepy Donna. In a way, that was funny. Usually kids woke up when something exciting happened, but Donna had looked as if she could hardly keep her eyes open. She hadn't even seemed interested.

Then there was Henry. Henry seldom showed by his face what he was thinking, but he had taken a willing part in the search. She looked at him, and he returned her gaze quietly and thoughtfully. Did *he*, like Mr. Gage, think she had rung the gong?

Celeste had gone back to bed, apparently convinced of the outcome of the search before it had started. Miss Twig was enjoying the excitement, and Mr. Bogardus had been helpful from the beginning. Mrs. Tuckerman had been the first to appear on the stairs and had been plainly upset.

There just weren't any suspects. Not one of these people could have hidden downstairs. This really was a mystery. David would have to do a lot of thinking to make anything of this.

Mrs. Saunders rose and straightened her shoulders. "We might as well all go back to bed."

Miss Hattie Twig waited for Taffy and Mrs. Saunders on the landing. "You know that bird was at my window again tonight a little after nine o'clock. I was tempted to open the window and see if it would fly in, but I didn't quite have the courage."

Back in her room, Taffy got quickly into bed and snuggled beneath the covers. There was still a reckoning she was not anxious to face. Her mother sat on the edge of the bed beside her, and she knew there were going to be questions she didn't want to answer.

"Now, then, Taffy, you'd better tell me just what you were doing on the stairs at that hour of the night. What in the world were you up to?"

Taffy turned over on her side so that she could look up into her mother's face. "I didn't ring the gong, mother. Honestly, I didn't."

"I never thought you did. It isn't the sort of malicious trick you'd play. But not everyone here knows you as well as I do. To say the least, it's unfortunate that you had to be caught in the middle of an affair like that. Suppose you tell me all about it."

Taffy had put the keys beneath her pillow. She could

feel the box there, a hard bump beneath the softness. If she told her mother about them now — told her about how she and David were working on the mysteries and how she had wanted to prove to David that she had just as much nerve as he had as far as that locked room was concerned — she knew pretty well what her mother's reaction would be.

"Were you hungry?" her mother prompted. "Were you going downstairs to get something to eat?"

That was an out, but somehow she couldn't take advantage of it. "No," she said, "I wasn't hungry."

"You couldn't have rung that gong without knowing it, I suppose?"

"Oh, mother! Of course not. I was perfectly wide awake." Maybe it *would* be better to tell the whole thing and stop these questions. "I did go downstairs for a reason. Sort of a — a secret reason. It wasn't anything wrong. Just something I wanted to find out about that — locked room. I wanted to see if I could open it and —"

Her mother's sigh had an exasperated sound. "Taffy! Not that again! The door is locked. Let it stay locked; I'll get to it in time. Of all the foolish ideas! Why would it be any more likely to be open in the middle of the night than in the daytime?"

Taffy was silent. There was no use trying to explain. Later on, of course, she would tell the whole story, but at the moment some other subject would be safer.

"Mother, what about that will of Aunt Martha's? What does it say? I mean, how will you know whether you'll get Sunset House or not?"

Mrs. Saunders got into bed and plumped up her pillows. "I have to run it for one summer with a profit equal to the average profits the hotel earned during the years when Aunt Martha managed it herself."

"But what happens to it if you don't?"

Mrs. Saunders reached toward the bed lamp and turned it off. "I don't know, honey. There's a sealed part to the will that isn't to be opened until the middle of September. I've told you that."

"Donna says her mother thinks some bird society will get it if you don't. Only Celeste doesn't think so. She thinks it will go to the Tuckermans."

"That's all talk, honey," her mother told her quickly. "You mustn't discuss things like that with Donna. I doubt if either Mrs. Tuckerman or Celeste knows a thing about it. Aunt Martha wasn't exactly a predictable person. She was more likely to do unexpected things, like suddenly willing the hotel to me. The only thing we need be concerned about is proving that Sunset House can go right on being successful in our hands."

"It's not doing so good now, is it?" Taffy asked. "The Gages are going to leave, and maybe some of the others will go. Do you think somebody who wanted it to fail could be playing all these tricks?"

Taffy caught a quiver of uncertainty in her mother's voice. "I don't know. I'd hate to believe anything like that. Let's not talk about it any more tonight. We're both awfully tired, and sometimes things look all wrong in the middle of the night. Promise me one thing, please? Don't get any more wonderful ideas that can't wait till morning to be carried out."

"I won't!" Taffy promised fervently. "But — mother, I wish daddy was here."

"I do too," her mother said. "Maybe running a hotel was biting off a bigger piece than I'm able to chew."

"Oh, no!" Taffy cried. She couldn't bear to hear her mother sound discouraged. Mother was always braver than anybody else. "You *can* do it! I *know* you can!"

Her mother's hand came out to squeeze hers in the darkness.

In the morning, when she went downstairs with her mother, Mrs. Tuckerman met them at the foot of the stairs, and held out a note.

"This is dreadful!" she said. "I don't know what we're going to do."

The note was from Celeste. She could not, she had written, work in a place that had been given so many warnings. If Mrs. Saunders was wise, she would close the hotel and move out, as she — Celeste — was doing immediately.

Taffy looked at her mother in alarm. But with morning her mother's spirit had come back. There was a light in her eyes, and Taffy felt reassured.

"Let Celeste go!" Mrs. Saunders said firmly. "She was becoming more trouble than she was worth. We'll pinchhit without her until we find a new cook. There's no reason why we can't get one who'll be a lot less superstitious and temperamental."

"I don't know —" Mrs. Tuckerman began doubtfully, but Mrs. Saunders was already on her way to the kitchen to talk to Celeste's assistant and see that breakfast went smoothly.

Taffy ran upstairs and hung the "red is for danger" sign in the window to summon David. Then she joined Donna at breakfast.

Donna was wide awake now and full of chatter about Celeste's leaving. Whatever was Mrs. Saunders going to do?

Taffy attempted an imitation of mother's own assurance. There were other cooks in the world. Sunset House would manage.

· Nevertheless, the pancakes weren't as good as usual; Celeste's pancakes were something to dream about. But at least the guests were not yet aware of Celeste's departure, and they didn't *all* eat pancakes.

After breakfast Taffy went upstairs and took Miss Irwin's journal from the drawer in her table. Then, on sudden impulse, she went in search of Mr. Bogardus.

She found him walking in the garden. "Hello," he said cheerfully, just as if there had been no midnight uproar.

Taffy held out the journal. "Remember what Miss Twig said about Aunt Martha writing everything in her journals? Well, there's something in this one about you."

The next moment she felt embarrassed and wished she had not been so sudden. Suppose he didn't want people to know he had proposed to Mrs. Tuckerman at Arch Rock. But he certainly ought to know what Miss Irwin had done to set Mrs. Tuckerman against him, because it was nonsense, of course.

He started to read and, after a moment, gave a low whistle and looked at her solemnly.

"It isn't true," she said loyally. "I mean about — about wanting the hotel and — "

He smiled. "I do want the hotel, but I'd want to buy it. I'd have bought it from Miss Irwin if she'd been willing to sell. If your mother inherits the hotel, and can then be persuaded to sell it to me — "

Taffy broke in excitedly. "Then if you asked Mrs. Tuckerman to marry you, she couldn't think it was because of the hotel."

Before Mr. Bogardus could answer, Mr. Gage's indignant voice drifted out from the hotel. Apparently he was giving Mrs. Saunders and Mrs. Tuckerman his final opinion of Sunset House before he and his wife left.

Taffy's excitement died. How could mother ever inherit the hotel the way things were going? "Do you know Celeste has left?" she asked.

Mr. Bogardus nodded. "I think," he said gravely, "we need to get to the bottom of some things."

David came around the hotel through the side yard, and

Taffy went to tell him about the affairs of the night.

"There I was with that horrid club thing in my hand," she said. " So now I guess *I'm* the chief suspect."

David shook his head. "Circumstantial evidence. That always comes into a mystery. It doesn't mean a thing. Mostly it throws suspicion the wrong way."

Taffy was doubtful. "What if the people who saw me don't know that? Anyway, this makes me want to solve the mystery all the more. Then they'll know I didn't put that bat in Miss Twig's bed, or ring the gong, or anything."

"What *were* you coming downstairs for in the middle of the night?" David asked.

Taffy took the keys from her pocket. "I found these in the attic yesterday. I thought last night would be a good time to try them on the locked room. And then the gong rang and spoiled everything."

"You mean you haven't even tried 'em yet? Well, come on! What are we waiting for?"

David, Taffy thought, had completely overlooked the important fact that she had been proving her courage last night. Suddenly she began to wonder if what she had done had been brave, or merely silly. Wasn't it always silly to try to show off? Anyway they could now try the keys together.

They went through the lounge and closed the office door behind them. David wanted to take the keys, but Taffy held them tightly.

"*I* found them," she said. "I get to open the door."

David gave in. " O. K. I guess that's fair."

Taffy picked out one bright piece of metal, wishing that her hands wouldn't shake with excitement. But though the key slipped into the lock, it would not turn. She tried another key, but it would not fit into the lock. That left five more tries to go.

"You'd better let me," David protested. "Or else stop shivering."

"I'm not shivering," Taffy said. Then, unexpectedly, unbelievably, a key slipped neatly into place and turned as smoothly as if it had been oiled. The door was unlocked.

Taffy looked at David wide-eyed, a little frightened now that she was on the verge of the unknown, and suddenly very glad to have him there.

She turned the knob and pushed open the door. Once more the stifling odor of moth balls met her.

CHAPTER
❧ 19 ❧
The Unknown

TAFFY stared into darkness until the faint edgings of daylight around closely drawn shades became clear. As her eyes grew accustomed to the faint light, shadowy forms took on shape. They were strange winged forms — birds. They hovered everywhere, sharp beaks pointing, here and there an eye glinting in what little light there was. Taffy put a shaking hand on David's arm, glad that she had not opened the room alone last night.

"Don't be scared," David said, sounding as though he was not entirely at ease. "They're not live birds. They're all stuffed ones."

He felt along the wall and found the light switch. From overhead a bulb dazzled them with a burst of light. Taffy's heart pounded, even though she saw that David was right. There were several dozen birds, each so beautifully mounted that it seemed about to take flight, or to cock its head in the saucy way it had known in life.

Many things began to come clear to Taffy. The books in the library had been moved to the attic to make room for these feathered creatures. This was what Aunt Martha had meant in the journal when she spoke of her skill. People had brought dead birds to her after island storms and she had preserved them in their natural poses.

That small, graceful bird with the red breast must be the red-breasted grosbeak of the journal. And there, under a globe of glass, was a tiny hummingbird, quiet now as it had never been quiet when alive. Of course, with her superstitions and imaginings, Celeste had not approved of Aunt Martha's hobby. Aunt Martha had said in her journal that Celeste believed some of the birds might be wicked manitos, and that by preserving them she was giving a home to evil spirits. That was the reason Celeste thought it good that the door was locked. She had wanted to throw the key away to delay the opening of the room so that the spirits would, as she said, " go to sleep."

For a moment Taffy's vivid imagination almost fooled her into thinking that the hummingbird had fluttered its wings. Was a manito going to escape? She gave herself a mental shake to put such nonsense out of her head.

This was the mystery. This was the treasure. These birds must have been very precious to Aunt Martha. She had spent hours in stuffing and mounting them and she would not want careless hands to disturb her handiwork.

Then, at the far end of the room, a standard caught Taffy's eye. It was like the others on which the birds were mounted, but this one was empty.

" Whew! " David said. " Let's get a window open. This smell is terrible! I suppose she used some kind of stuff to keep the moths from getting at her birds. I thought they used preservatives on skins, but it looks like your aunt tossed in moth balls for good measure." He went to a window and reached for the shade pull. Then he said, "Hey — look! "

Taffy turned from the empty standard and saw that the cord to the shade was caught beneath the closed window.

" I thought you said you tried all these windows from the outside! " David said. " I thought you said they were all locked! "

" They were; every one of them."

" This one's not. Anybody'd have a hard time getting a

hand behind that caught shade to lock it. Wait a minute —
let's see if I can get it open."

He had to work awkwardly around the shade, but the
unlocked window pushed upward after a moment and the
shade, released, flew to the top. A current of air freshened
the room.

Taffy was puzzled. "How do you suppose the window
got unlocked, and then shoved down on the cord?"

David shook his head. "I don't know. Unless somebody
got out through it, crawling under the shade, and then
closed the window from the outside and caught the shade
cord.

"Somebody got out —" Taffy stared at him.

Now she knew what had happened last night. The person who had banged the gong had a key to the room. He'd
let himself into it, locked the door on the inside, and then
crawled out through the window. That meant it had to
be somebody on the outside and not any of the people in
the hotel, because nobody could have gone out through the
window and then come down the inside stairs. With the
doors locked, there was no way to get back into the house.

Taffy went thoughtfully to the empty standard. "Look,
David," she said, pointing to three feathers on the stand —
three feathers of silver gray.

"I think there was a bird here," she went on. "I think
it was a sea gull. And I don't think it was fixed up as well
as some of the others. Maybe Aunt Martha hadn't had
much practice when she mounted it because its feathers
seem to have fallen out. I found one stuck in the door that
day — remember? And yesterday I found one in the attic.
I thought it was the one of Grayfeather's that Henry had
given Donna."

David nodded calmly. "I guess maybe you're right.
There was a bird there."

Taffy continued to look thoughtfully at the standard.

"You know something, David? I'll bet I have the answer to the mystery of the gulls. And I'll bet I know what we can do about it."

David's calmness left him. "Well, creepers, tell me!"

She told him very slowly and carefully, because she was thinking aloud as she went along, outlining the plan that had come to her.

"I won't do anything mother wouldn't like this time," she said. "I'll get permission to stay up a little while longer tonight. Of course I'll have to see if Miss Twig will help. I think she will. I think she'll love it."

"She could be an accomplice," David said eagerly. Then, "No, an accomplice is usually on the criminal's side." Suddenly he put his hands to his head and moved it from side to side. "Everything's going to happen — and I won't be here! I won't be in at the finish at all."

"Maybe your grandmother would let you stay all night," Taffy said hopefully. "We could put up a cot for you downstairs."

They closed and locked the window and pulled down the shade. Quietly they let themselves out of the room that was a mystery no longer and locked the door. Taffy tied a piece of string to the right key so she would know which one belonged to the door.

As they were leaving the office Mr. Bogardus came in from the garden. "Where is Celeste?" he asked. "I must see her at once."

"She's gone," Taffy reminded him.

"Then we must find out where she's gone. Someone ought to know."

"Doris might," Taffy said. "What is it? What's happened?"

"This!" Mr. Bogardus held up the journal she had given him. "I've learned something pretty interesting. Ask Doris, will you?"

A reading table and a standing ash tray rocked peril-
ously as Taffy hurried off. Doris was upstairs in her own
room in the employees' wing, painting her nails. She gave
the name and address of the friend Celeste had gone to
visit, and five minutes later David, Taffy, and Mr. Bogardus were all on the way to the back street above the
village. It was only a short walk, during which Mr. Bogardus kept snapping his fingers, ignoring Taffy's eager
questions. The house they sought was a small house, neatly
kept. The woman who let them in showed them to a living
room and left them there. A few minutes later Celeste
came to the doorway and stood looking at them unhappily.

" No," she said flatly before anyone could speak. " I will
not go back. Never. That is my final decision."

" Oh, we didn't come about that," Mr. Bogardus told
her cheerfully. " Mrs. Saunders is getting another cook.
There wouldn't be a place for you."

Celeste's astonishment was plain.

" After all," Mr. Bogardus continued, " people must eat.
Mrs. Saunders must get another cook. What else did you
think she'd do? "

" She thought we'd just close up," Taffy burst out. " She
thought we couldn't run without her."

Celeste said: " She will close. There is no other way."

" Sit down, Celeste," Mr. Bogardus invited. " Now, let's
have a sensible look at this thing. If Mrs. Saunders is
forced to close the hotel, do you know what will happen to
it according to Miss Irwin's will? "

" Mrs. Saunders will not get it," Celeste said quickly, as
if there were satisfaction in the thought. She had seated
herself on the edge of the sofa next to Taffy.

" And we won't be able to buy our own house! " Taffy
wailed. " And I'll never, never have my own room."

Celeste threw her a quick look. " Everything cannot

work out well for everyone."

"If Mrs. Saunders doesn't get Sunset House," Mr. Bogardus asked, "what will happen to it?"

"It will go to Mrs. Tuckerman," Celeste said with conviction. "Of that I am sure. Then the little girl, Donna, will have her chance as a dancer and it will all be just and fair."

"And if it doesn't go to Mrs. Tuckerman?" Mr. Bogardus asked.

"You mean it might go to the bird society?" Celeste brooded. "No, that is not like Miss Irwin. She left them money. She wanted Sunset House to go on being a hotel, so who else would get it but Mrs. Tuckerman?" The cook made an impatient gesture. "All this is just guessing."

Mr. Bogardus held up the book. "Not quite, Celeste. I have Martha Irwin's journal here in which she wrote out her plans quite fully. She was capable of playing rather queer pranks on people. Let me read you something she wrote."

Taffy waited breathlessly while Mr. Bogardus found the page.

"'Sarah Tuckerman,'" he read, "'has become more and more difficult lately. She is pouring all her interest out upon her child, and Donna is growing spoiled. Under no circumstances will I leave the hotel to Sarah in my will.

"'It might be amusing to leave Sunset House to Betty Saunders — or at least to tantalize her with it to punish her for her heartless behavior toward me after I had done so much for her as a girl. I wish I could be here to witness the comedy when Betty attempts to make a success of running a hotel. Of course she will snarl things; she has a gift for snarling things.'"

"That's not one bit true," Taffy cried indignantly. "I don't think Aunt Martha was a very nice person."

"I'm inclined to agree with you," Mr. Bogardus said

dryly, and continued reading. "'So — I will play a wry joke on the lot of them. I will leave the hotel to my one good, true, trusted friend. I will leave it to Celeste Cloutier.'"

Taffy and David stared at Celeste. The cook's face went blank with surprise.

"What would I do with a hotel?" she demanded.

"A hotel could be a very fine thing to own," Mr. Bogardus said. "It would mean a good income. With a possibility like this open, it might be worth anyone's while to see that the hotel did not go to Mrs. Saunders."

Celeste's dark eyes took fire and she came to her feet. "You mean I would *try* to make things difficult for Mrs. Saunders so that the hotel would come to *me?* You think I could do a thing like that? You say that to me?"

Mr. Bogardus said gently: "You've been helping it along that road, haven't you? You've been going on strike and spreading stories of Indian spirits."

Celeste sank back on the sofa. "But that was because I wanted it to go to the Tuckermans. That is where it belongs in fairness. What do *I* want with a hotel? All the bother and the trouble and the worry! I could not for two minutes be a hotel manager."

"You could sell it," Mr. Bogardus suggested. "It would bring enough money to keep you comfortably for the rest of your days. You wouldn't have to cook any more."

Celeste's head came up in dismay. "But that is my life! Owning a hotel — poof! And what do I want with money to keep me in idleness? I have saved what I need. I can earn more. This must not happen. I won't have it."

"It doesn't need to happen, Celeste," Mr. Bogardus said. "All you have to do is come back to the hotel and help Mrs. Saunders by serving the sort of meals only you can cook."

Taffy watched him in admiration. She could see just how

cunningly he was coaxing Celeste to return to Sunset House and save the day. He *was* nice. He was wonderful.

But Celeste shook her head unhappily. " I would like to go. If it is not to be for Mrs. Tuckerman, then I would gladly help Mrs. Saunders. I like her and I like this girl Taffy. But I cannot do it."

" Why not, Celeste? " Taffy cried. " If you help mother out, then we'll get the hotel and we do need the money terribly. Mr. Bogardus will buy it, and if Mrs. Tuckerman marries him — " She knew she shouldn't be babbling about Mr. Bogardus' affairs but she couldn't stop. " Then Donna can have her training as a dancer. Don't you see? You'll cook at Sunset House forever and ever. And we can have *our* house."

" Creepers! " David said. " Everything will be swell."

Mr. Bogardus smiled. "Taffy moves a bit quickly, but I think she's on the right road. How about it, Celeste? "

Celeste had the tragic look of one about to cry. " Oh, I *would* like to! I would like more than anything to have all these good things come about. But I cannot."

" Why, Celeste? " Taffy pleaded. " Whyever can't you? "

" Because of the wings," Celeste sighed. " Because Sunset House has been taken over by an evil manito. Gulls at the windows; spirit birds warning and threatening; wings against the gong in the middle of the night; bones hiding in a bed. No — I cannot go back."

" It isn't spirits," Taffy kept on. " It's a person. Sometimes I've even thought it might be you. If we can show that it isn't a spirit, but a real person, will you come back? "

Celeste looked alarmed. " It is dangerous to trap a manito. It can do you harm."

" But if it isn't a manito — if we can prove it isn't? "

Celeste could not be moved. " The birds do not like Sunset House any more. They do not like you or your mother. It is not the way it was when Miss Irwin was alive. I did not like all that she did, but I knew the good manitos would protect her. You have no protection."

Mr. Bogardus closed what appeared to be turning into a useless, discouraging wrangle. " Anyway, you have something to think over, Celeste. And whether you want to own a hotel or not, it looks as if one might be coming to you, headaches, evil spirits, and all."

Outside Taffy drew a deep breath of fresh, clear Mackinac air. " Why does she have to be so silly and stubborn, Uncle Jerry? Does she really believe in manitos? "

" I sometimes think she does," Mr. Bogardus said. " Or else she is a very good actress and is fooling us all. There doesn't seem to be anything we can do to change her mind — at least, not right now."

" Maybe by tomorrow we can change it," David said. " Maybe."

Mr. Bogardus gave him a sidelong glance. " Sounds as though you kids have something up your sleeves. Wouldn't care to tell me about it, would you? "

Taffy and David exchanged looks and David gave the faintest shake of his head.

" We'd rather not talk about it yet," Taffy said. She knew she could trust Uncle Jerry, but it seemed better that their plan should remain secret.

Again the day was a long day of waiting, this time for the hour to lay a trap for the mysterious " spirit " of Sunset House.

CHAPTER

❧ 20 ❦

Spirit Trap

B<small>Y</small> NINE o'clock that night the trap was ready. Miss Twig had been brought into the plot. She knew the part she was to play, and was almost breathless with anticipation. Mrs. Marsh had given David permission to spend the night at the hotel, and Mrs. Saunders had agreed to set up a cot for him downstairs, though neither woman could understand the excitement that surrounded David's overnight visit. Since she had a guest, Taffy had little difficulty in winning permission to stay up later.

David's arrival brought an unexpected complication. With him came Grayfeather in the familiar traveling hatbox.

"I didn't want to leave him alone for so long a time," David explained to Taffy. "Will it be all right if he stays here tonight?"

When she was consulted, Mrs. Saunders sighed and agreed that, though sea gulls were not her favorite birds at the moment, it would probably be all right if this bird stayed for one night. Taffy raided the kitchen for leftovers and the gull ate greedily. Then he was fastened to a perch in the garden out of sight of the veranda.

Now Taffy and David were in Miss Twig's room, discussing the plan in whispers.

"Do you suppose we'd better turn out the light?" Miss Twig asked, patting at a flying miller that darted in the wide-open window.

" I don't think so," Taffy said. " The bird always comes to lighted windows. It's supposed to be seen and to frighten people."

"What if it doesn't come tonight?" David asked anxiously. " It would be just my luck. You can try this again, but I can't stay here every night."

" I think —" Miss Twig began and then gave a little whisper of excitement.

A gull, its wings outstretched, was swooping back and forth before the window. It was much bigger than Grayfeather, and its eyes gleamed wickedly in the lamplight.

But there was no time for watching the bird. Miss Twig knew the part she had to play and Taffy and David knew what they must do.

David got to the door first, but Taffy's dash down the upper hallway was speedier than his. She was first on the attic stairs, padding softly upward, with David at her heels. They reached the attic, and Taffy's hand found the ladder to the trap door in the roof.

As they'd expected, the trap door stood open.

Triumph ran through Taffy. The spirit was caught above them, trapped for sure. Even though Miss Twig, reaching out the window for the bird, would warn the person on the roof of danger, he still could not get away except down the ladder, and they had the ladder guarded.

Taffy climbed fast. She reached the trap door and went through it out onto the widow's walk that topped the house. The moon had gone behind a cloud, but the stars gave enough light to make out the railing around the walk. It was empty. There was no " spirit" to be captured. Beyond the railed walk, the roofs pitched down at various angles on all sides and the roofs were empty too.

" No one could get away," Taffy cried. " No one could possibly get away."

But someone had. Either into thin air — if there were

spirits — or over the slanting roofs of Sunset House, if it were someone human.

The answer became clear to Taffy. Down those slanting heights lay the only way of escape, and only one person could have taken that way. Only one person would have chosen such a perilous way. It had to be the boy who could run out across the narrow, high-flung bridge of Arch Rock. It had to be Henry Fox.

"I didn't *want* it to be Henry," Taffy almost wept. "I didn't want it to be!"

"I guess that's who it was all right." David sounded as sorry as she was. "Maybe we know now what happened the other night when the gong was banged."

Taffy could see it clearly enough. Henry had let himself into the locked room and climbed out through a window. Then he had gone up the tree whose branches touched the roof — a tree she had once seen him in — and climbed the roof to the widow's walk. From there he had let himself into the house and mingled with the guests coming downstairs.

"Well," David said, "we can't do anything here. We'd better go back and see what's happened to Miss Twig."

They met her at the door of her room. Her arms were triumphantly full of stuffed sea gull and her hair was full of feathers.

"I caught it!" she cried. "You can see all the cords and wires and things that were used to let it down over the edge of the roof."

It took a few minutes to separate Miss Twig from feathers and cords.

"Did you catch the spirit?" she asked anxiously. "Surely you didn't let him get away!"

"We didn't see him," Taffy said. "He ran down over the roof."

"But we think we know who it was," David added.

Footsteps sounded on the stairs. Looking down the hall, Taffy saw Mr. Bogardus and Henry. The habitual smile was gone from Uncle Jerry's face and Henry was no longer the inscrutable Indian, but a frightened boy.

"Within the past five minutes," Mr. Bogardus said, "I've been putting two and two together. I stepped out of the hotel in time to see Miss Twig catch a bird and haul it into her room, and then I caught Henry coming off the roof."

"Henry!" Taffy cried. "How could you do such an awful thing?"

He looked away from her without answering.

Down the hall a door opened softly. Taffy knew the sound; it was one of the first sounds she had heard at Sunset House. But this time Donna did not close the door and go into hiding. She came out of her room and looked at the bird in Miss Twig's arms, then at a stern Mr. Bogardus, and last of all at Henry.

"It isn't *his* fault," she said, coming toward the group. "I made him do it."

"But *why?*" Taffy wailed. "Why did you want to hurt us? How could you be so mean?"

"Donna," Mr. Bogardus said, both sternness and gentleness in his voice, "please go and get your mother. And, Taffy —"

But Taffy had no need to go for her mother. Mrs. Saunders had come up the stairs and was in the hall.

"There's our spirit bird," Mr. Bogardus said, nodding toward Miss Twig and her captive. "It's one Miss Irwin had in her collection. Henry has been letting it down from the roof at night to disturb the guests, apparently at Donna's instigation."

Taffy saw her mother's lips tighten. "Perhaps we'd better have a talk downstairs, all of us, and get to the bottom of this." She led the way to Aunt Martha's office, where

Donna and Mrs. Tuckerman joined them.

"We can talk in here," Mrs. Saunders said. Two bright spots of color burned in her cheeks.

A worried Mrs. Tuckerman pushed Donna ahead of her into the office. Miss Twig gave the gull to Mr. Bogardus and hurried away, as if the mystery had become something that was no longer fun. At the door of the office Taffy found herself stopped by her mother.

"No, honey. This is something Mrs. Tuckerman and Uncle Jerry and I — and of course Donna and Henry — have to talk over alone."

Taffy stared at her mother in dismay. "You mean, right at the end of the mystery — "

"Taffy!" Mrs. Saunders said, and Taffy knew better than to argue.

Disappointed, she watched the office door close upon the others. After all, she and David and Miss Twig had been the ones to solve the mystery. They had a *right* to be in that room at the finish.

"I guess maybe your mother's right," David said out of the silence. "If you and I had been up to something, we wouldn't want half the town in to hear about it. Maybe Henry and Donna can talk better if we're not there."

Taffy tossed her head. "If they're practically — practically *juvenile delinquents,* I don't see why — "

"I like Henry," David said.

Taffy sighed. "I do too. And most of the time I like Donna. But how can we like them now?"

"I give up," David said. "Let's go out and see Grayfeather."

They went down the steps of the rear veranda and across the lawn. The sky had cleared and the night was silver. Halfway through the garden, Taffy put a hand on David's arm.

"Look! Down there on the rocks beside the water. It's Celeste."

They crossed the grass softly and the woman on the rocks seemed unaware of their presence.

"Celeste!" Taffy called. "Oh, Celeste, you've come back!"

The cook lifted her head. "Only to think. Only to see if I can find a way."

"But there *is* a way," Taffy said. "The mystery is over now. There wasn't any spirit bird. It was only a stuffed gull from Aunt Martha's bird room. Henry was letting it down before the windows on a wire. Donna says she made him do it."

Celeste shook her head unhappily. "Then it was a manito made *them* do it. An evil manito."

"Oh, Celeste!" Taffy cried in exasperation. "I don't know why they did it, but they did it. You can come back to the hotel now. There won't be any more trouble."

But Celeste's thoughts were now with Donna and Henry. "Perhaps I talked too much to them. Donna is one of great imagination. If I could believe it is really over — if I thought the gulls once more had a fondness for Sunset House —"

"*Then* would you come back?" Taffy asked, an undertone of excitement in her voice.

"If I could believe that, yes. Then I would come back. I am not happy away from Sunset House, but —"

"Wait!" Taffy cried. "Wait right here!"

She caught David by the arm, pulled him away, out of Celeste's hearing, and whispered hurriedly. Then she was off across the lawn, running toward the kitchen.

The last plate had been washed, the last pot had been cleaned, and the spotless kitchen was empty. Taffy switched on a light and went to the cupboard where the canned foods were kept. She found what she wanted and got out a can opener. Then she turned off the light and hurried back to Celeste. David had gone to get Grayfeather. The bird cocked his head at them and ruffled his wings fretfully as though he did not like being disturbed.

But his attitude changed the moment Taffy picked a drippy sardine from the tin and dangled it above his bill. He took it down with a gulp and came wide awake.

"All right," Taffy said to David. "Let's see if it will work."

She was worried now, but she tried not to show it as she stepped up on the rocks beside Celeste. After all, the young gull knew David a lot better then he knew her. If this plan failed, they might lose Celeste for good. It was *so* important that she come back to Sunset House cheerfully and willingly. More than anything else, the hotel needed Celeste.

"Celeste," Taffy said, and her voice sounded very small. "I want to prove something to you. I want to show you that the gulls really do like the Saunderses and Sunset House."

She held up the tin of sardines. David had released Grayfeather and suddenly the gull circled into the air. There was nothing wrong with his wings now, and he seemed to have regained confidence in his own flying ability. Above their heads he soared and swooped, triumphantly glad to be free, one with the sea and air again.

He came down to the water with a long glide and rested on the surface not far from shore. Had they lost him for good right when they needed him most, Taffy thought with a sinking heart. She jiggled the sardine tin and called his name over and over again.

"Grayfeather! Look what I've got for you, Grayfeather."

She had given up hope when he rose from the water, soared, circled their heads twice, and glided down to her shoulder. She felt his wet claws through her blouse, but did not flinch as she held the tin up where he could reach it. Eagerly he leaned from her shoulder to pick fish from the can. When the tin was empty, he perched for a moment longer on her shoulder with no show of fear. Then he rose and soared out across the water. As he disappeared in the moonlight, Taffy heard again the mewing cry which had been her first introduction to the gulls of Mackinac Island. She faced Celeste happily.

"Do you hear that? He isn't calling for help. He's calling, 'Hello! Hello!' He's our friend, Celeste. And he's going back to tell the others how well he's been treated at Sunset House."

Celeste got slowly to her feet and stood looking out over the water. Presently, without a word, she started across the lawn.

"Where are you going?" Taffy called after her.

"To bed," Celeste tossed over her shoulder. "A good breakfast for Sunset House means a good night's sleep first."

She was humming, and the sound came back through the night. The tune was the *voyageurs'* song.

When she was out of sight, Taffy whirled herself around in a dizzy circle. "We've won, David! We've won! Grayfeather and us!"

Over in the hotel a light snapped off in Aunt Martha's office and Taffy stopped her dance.

"I guess they're through talking," David said.

Soberly the two walked toward the hotel veranda. Even though there would be no more trouble at Sunset House, and even though Celeste would be back in the kitchen tomorrow, Taffy's spirits were suddenly dampened. There was still Henry and Donna. In spite of everything, she liked them, and she knew they had got themselves into serious trouble.

CHAPTER

21

An End to Mystery

IT WAS much later than Taffy was usually allowed to stay up, but she would make up for lost sleep in the morning. She sat up in bed, a pillow propped behind her, and watched her mother, who sat at the window.

She had been half afraid that mother would get right into bed and turn off the lights, and there were many questions she wanted to ask. But mother sat at the window as if she intended to remain there for some time.

"Why did Donna and Henry do what they did?" Taffy asked hopefully. "How *could* they?"

For a while Mrs. Saunders stared out at the starlit garden of Sunset House. "We have to go back a little," she said at last, "to understand just how it was. There must have been times when Mrs. Tuckerman was very lonely at Sunset House. Guests came and went, and she had no close friends. Probably she talked to Donna about us, and about Aunt Martha and the will, long before we came to Mackinac. I think she was hurt because Aunt Martha left the hotel to a niece she hadn't seen in years."

"I suppose I wouldn't have liked our coming here, if I'd been in Donna's place," Taffy said.

"It wasn't only not liking our coming here. I think that without meaning to, or without quite realizing what she was doing, Mrs. Tuckerman made Donna feel that we would be to blame if she had to give up her dancing because of lack of money."

Taffy remembered the first day at lunch when Donna had spoken so intensely about her ambition to be a dancer.

"I'm sure Mrs. Tuckerman never intended to injure us. I don't believe she realized the ideas she was putting into the mind of her daughter. Donna had also listened to Celeste, and was ready to blame us for everything."

"Sometimes I thought she liked me," Taffy said wistfully.

"She does like you, but she was all mixed up inside. I don't mean that we can excuse what she did, but she isn't really wicked, any more than Henry is wicked. Imaginations are fine, but they have to be properly directed or they get people into all kinds of trouble."

That was a little frightening, Taffy thought. *She* had an imagination.

But even as she thought about it, she knew that she might do foolish things sometimes, like every other boy and girl, but that she'd never try to hurt anyone. And she knew why. Looking across the room at her mother, she felt a soft welling up of affection inside her.

Mrs. Saunders went on with the story. "Donna had no plan, though she was behind the scare Henry gave you in the wood. Then came the storm and the gull that crashed through the Twigs' window. When she saw how upset the Twigs became, she got the idea of frightening them into leaving, and enlisted Henry's help."

"But why would Henry want to help her?" Taffy asked. "He couldn't have had anything against us."

Mrs. Saunders sighed. "He had a reason that looked right to him at the time, though I think he understands now how wrong it was. Once when Aunt Martha got one of her mind-changing spells, she decided not to help Henry with money to study medicine. But Mrs. Tuckerman stepped in and saved things for Henry. Donna used that. She pointed out that here was a chance for Henry to repay her mother."

"I'll bet he didn't really want to do it," Taffy said quickly.

"I don't think he wanted to, but there was no one looking after him except Celeste, and she had more queer ideas than anyone else. Anyway, when Donna said she wished they could get into the bird room and see what they might use, Henry told her he knew where Celeste had hidden the key after Aunt Martha's death. He went out to the Cannon Ball and got it, substituting another key in its place."

"What about the bat bones in Miss Twig's bed?"

"That was Donna's doing. She didn't stop there. You remember the night you and she slept downstairs in the office?"

Taffy nodded eagerly. "So it *was* Donna that night! She got the sandwiches to fool me. Then she turned off the lights and went into the locked room."

"And removed the stuffed gull from its standard," Mrs. Saunders said. "When you came to the door and opened it, she thought she was caught, but you ran off toward the stairs and she locked the door and hid the gull under her cot. Then she stopped you from waking the house."

Taffy saw the whole picture now. It made her a little angry to think how easily she'd been fooled and frightened, and yet at the same time there was a feeling of regret for Donna.

"As guests began to leave the hotel," her mother continued, "Henry grew worried. I believe he sincerely liked us. But the trouble with starting something wrong is that it's so hard to end it. He and Donna quarreled the day of the trip to Arch Rock, but Donna promised that if he'd help a little longer, the whole thing would be over. The story Uncle Jerry told about the gong gave her another idea."

Again Taffy nodded. " I know. It was Henry, wasn't it, who took the war club and banged the gong? And he got away through the locked room and up over the roof."

" That's right. And, of course, it was Henry who let the gull down before the windows. But all the ideas were Donna's."

" What's going to happen to them? " Taffy asked. And she added, " It seems awful."

" It is awful," Mrs. Saunders agreed. " I think they realize that fully now. But, like anyone who does wrong, they'll have to take their punishment."

" What punishment? "

" Uncle Jerry thought the best thing would be to let them pick their own punishment. Donna is going to give up for a while — the thing she cares most about — her dancing. And I know Henry will pick something equally hard for himself."

" I suppose I can't play with them any more? " Taffy asked wistfully.

" Of course you can. Right at this moment they need friends. Not snooty, superior friends — just friends."

" What about Uncle Jerry? " Taffy asked, relieved. " Do you think he'll buy the hotel? "

" I'm sure he will."

" And what about Mrs. Tuckerman? "

" Turn off the light and come here," Mrs. Saunders whispered over her shoulder.

Taffy obeyed and went to stand beside her mother at the window. Down in the garden two people were walking — a rather tall woman and a plump little man.

" Donna needs a father," Mrs. Saunders said. " And I think with Uncle Jerry here at the hotel looking after things, Henry Fox will have a better chance to grow into a fine young man. Now then — back to bed you go! Not another question, not another word! "

Taffy wanted to stay there by the window and watch Mrs. Tuckerman and Uncle Jerry. And she certainly didn't want to stop talking—not for the whole night. But mother's voice had a mother sound that she understood. She scooted across the room, jumped into bed, and pulled the covers up around her ears.

She was glad tonight that she had that mother sound to listen to. It was something to make everything balance right; it was something sure, to trust and to hold onto.

Tomorrow would be a new day on Mackinac Island — an untroubled day, with wonderful trails to follow and new sights to see. Ahead, in the distant September, there would be Chicago and daddy again, and the day when all three Saunderses would be living together in a home of their own.

It was good, Taffy thought, to have an end to mystery.